ALSO BY LAURA DALEO

Immortal Kiss

Bound by Blood

The Vampire Within

The Vow

The Soul Collector

The Doll

My Name Is Death

Once We Were Witches

By

Laura Daleo

AUTHOR LAURA DALEO

Once We Were Witches is a work of fiction. Names, characters, places, and incidents either are the product of the author's imagination or are used fictitiously. Any resemblance to actual persons living or dead, events, or locales is entirely coincidental.

Published in the United States by Author Laura Daleo, Tucson, Arizona

Print ISBN: 978-1-7366103-2-9

ebook ISBN: 978-1-7366103-3-6

Chapter 1

A breaking news alert flashed on the TV screen as I bit into my bagel.

As the reporter stood by, the camera panned over to the lifeless body of a young woman hanging from a tree branch. The word witch was carved into her gray, bloodstained forehead. He sighed and hung his head. "A seventh victim has been added to the list."

I shoved my bagel aside as a sick feeling gripped my stomach. My heart ached as I stared at the girl's lifeless face. How could someone be so cruel and sadistic? This was not just a random act of cruelty. And where were the police in all of this?

My mom walked in, grabbed the remote, and shut off the TV.

"I was watching that."

"There's no need to watch some sicko murder young women. Life's too short to fixate on people like that."

"I'm not fixated," I clarified. "I'm concerned. There's a difference. That's seven girls now. Each with the word witch carved into their foreheads. What are the police doing? Nothing?"

She blew me off. "Investigations take time. The police are doing everything they can. Your dad and I see a lot of accidents at the hospital. Sadly, crime is a real thing. But you," she kissed my forehead, "don't need to worry about that. Your focus should be on college and the class you need to get to."

Mom was wrong. I had to worry. The creep pursued young women, specifically witches, a trait I shared and kept to myself. While my parents were blue-eyed and blonde-haired, I had pitch-black hair and brown eyes, and I also had strange birthmarks covering my forearms. It might seem like I have a tragic story, but I believe everything happens for a reason. Maybe I was destined to be abandoned outside the hospital where my adoptive parents worked. As they headed home after a long shift, they heard a faint cry near the emergency entrance. Rushing to investigate, they found me abandoned on the front steps, bundled in a pink blanket. As fate would have it, they immediately took me in and showered me with love.

As a baby, a toddler, a teen, and now at 19, a college student, they never saw me as anything but sweet, curious, sulky, and smart. They had no idea what I was hiding, the power I perfected, the spells I practiced, the magic I shed. In their eyes, I was like them. I knew I was someone beyond their comprehension, someone powerful. But who was I? Who were my birth parents who should have taught me how to use the gifts given to me at birth? The only information I had about my past came from visions—an image of a dark figure dropping me outside the hospital. There were no records of my birth, my parents, a location—as if I never existed. Bringing my questions to my adoptive parents wouldn't do any good. They'd kept these secrets hidden from me. In spite of me knowing the real truth, my adoptive parents provided a birth certificate, giving me the name, Raven Sagestone. I love them, but I want answers. I wanted to know the truth, and it was clear it wouldn't come from them. This was something I had to figure out for myself.

I put on my cropped denim jacket, kissed my mom on the cheek, and hit up Uber on my cell. My driver's tests were a total disaster. I failed every time. It creeped me out when the instructors stared at me with their beady eyes. So...my driver's license was out, and Uber was in. Having someone else do all the driving was a much better plan, for now anyway.

Forty minutes before class, the Uber driver dropped me off in front of the massive steps leading up to entrance of Granite Bay University. It was one of the oldest schools in Jodence, like something straight out of a fairytale. Its structure was reminiscent of a castle, with its towering columns, decorative arched windows, and cone-shaped roof; yet modern-day people dressed in jeans, T-shirts, and sneakers surrounded the ancient building—me being one of them.

In the past fourteen weeks, my daily agenda had consisted of visiting the library before class and researching its extensive collection of witchcraft, magic, and supernatural books. One of those books was certain to contain the answers to my birthright. I absorbed every word I came across about soul-bending, mental conjuring, healing rituals, protection rituals, binding magic, and the lore of fire, water, and air. One of the most fascinating things I discovered was the witch's mark. It has likely been around for hundreds, if not thousands, of years. However, between the 15th and 18th centuries, it had a much darker history than it does now. Witches were often burned, hanged, drowned, and tortured, and those with red hair and extra fingers and toes were often suspected of witchcraft. Witch hunters used moles, birthmarks, scars, and extra digits to identify witches. It was a myth that a particular god or bloodline was associated with the presence of a mole cluster or rose-colored mark. My arms were covered in black symbols like ancient ink, and neither a cluster nor a mark applied to me. Thank goodness I wasn't born back then.

With my arms full of books, I walked beneath the library's massive brick archways, combing its numerous aisles for books I hadn't read. When I rounded the corner, I tripped over a guy sitting on the floor. My books flew through the air and landed with a thud. I groaned as I hit the ground, hoping I had not damaged my books. The guy on the floor, on the other hand, quickly sprang up and apologized profusely.

His hands steadied me as he blurted, "Whoa, sorry." He helped me gather my books and ensured I was okay. An adorable smile swept along his lips as he brushed sandy-brown hair out of his hazel-colored eyes. He was probably one of those guys unaware of how cute he was, but cute or not, he'd parked his ass in the middle of the aisle, causing me to trip.

"What the hell, dude? There are tables to sit at and read."

"Yeah, I see your point," he grinned, revealing dimpled cheeks as he flipped through the books. "So you're into witches? Or maybe it's research for a paper about what's going now right now?"

"Does it matter?"

He squished his eyebrows together and tilted his head to the side. "Do you know my sister?"

"Huh?"

"Never mind." He tucked the books under his arm and bobbed his chin toward the tables. "Here, let me help you. It's the least I can do."

With a smile, I accepted his offer. "Thank you."

He arranged the books on the table before shoving his hands into his pockets. Then he stood there, studying me.

"Stare much?"

"Has anyone told you, you're difficult?" He didn't wait for me to respond. "But hey, I apologize for staring." He spread his fingers and moved them in a circular motion over my face. "You remind me of someone, Eve. She's got the same dark hair, ivory skin, and red lip look."

I shrugged. "I don't know anyone named Eve."

"Hmph."

The sound of a distant scream sent chills down my spine. My eyes darted around, searching for the source. "Did you hear that?"

"That was definitely a scream."

Students leapt from their seats, hurling books onto the floor as their gazes swept the room. Librarians abandoned their posts and spilled into the aisles. Panicked voices shouted, "Who screamed?" "What happened?" Me and the guy were thrown into madness by a stampede of people charging to the exits and pushing us out of the building and onto the library's steps.

As people fled in all directions, a storm of fear swept through the air. The sound of their footsteps pounding the sidewalks echoed in my ears. Backpacks sat abandoned on the ground, while others snapped pictures with their phones. As the chaos engulfed me, I trembled and struggled to catch my breath. The frantic faces around me mimicked my own fear as my eyes darted between them.

"There!" The guy pointed toward the sculpture of the university's tower in the courtyard.

I gasped as my eyes landed on the bodies. With their necks bound together, three girls covered in blood hung from the white tower. As I looked at their lifeless eyes and saw the word witch carved across their foreheads, a chill ran down my spine. An eerie, tragic, and horrific scene surrounded the bloodstained white tower. Students and teachers huddled together, whispering in disbelief, as the shrill of sirens echoed in the distance. The addition of three more innocent lives added pressure on the police to find those responsible.

"Damn, three this time," the guy uttered with shock.

I couldn't speak. My throat swelled with a huge sob as I slowly shook my head.

The police rushed in, their footsteps pounding the sidewalk as they raced toward the tower. They took samples, measured, photographed, and meticulously documented everything as they blocked off the area.

An officer, wearing an exasperated expression, yelled. "Get back! This is a crime scene."

I flinched, staggered backward, before firmly planting my feet on the ground. I wasn't going anywhere. This was my battle. I needed answers. Those poor girls needed answers too. My eyes narrowed as I demanded, "Why don't you find this sick creep before we all die?"

The guy's gaze burned into my flesh as he snapped his head toward me. "What are you doing?"

The officer thrust his shoulders back and barked out, "You need to step back."

"Are you trying to get arrested?" the guy whispered in my ear.

Just as his words entered my head, I overheard someone say, "They're ice cold; not a drop of blood in them."

My eyes locked on the authoritative policeman. "Blood? Is that new? Were the other girls drained of blood too?"

A pair of squinted eyes glared at me. "You can retreat or go downtown and think about your actions in a jail cell."

"Omgeez, man up much?" the guy said as he grabbed my arm and hurried me away. "You need to calm down."

I tore my gaze away from the dead girls and locked it on him. "Don't tell me what to do. You don't know anything about me. I want answers for those girls." *And myself,* I privately declared. "It seems nobody is fighting for them."

"It might seem that way on the surface, but I'm sure they're doing everything they can to help."

"I wish I could believe that, but dead bodies keep showing up..." My voice cracked as the sob squeezing my throat broke free. My shoulders quivered, and I buried my face in my hands.

He wrapped his arm around my shoulders and softened his voice. "They'll catch 'em. It'll be okay."

Sniffling, I sighed, "I can't concentrate. I can't be in class."

"We can walk to The Grind, get a coffee, and just relax." I nodded and let him lead me away from the gruesome scene of dead girls.

Chapter 2

An industrial vibe characterized The Grind—concrete counters, a black chalkboard displaying the menu, and exposed pipes on the ceiling adorned the mid-sized shop. While he ordered our drinks, I snagged one of the wooden tables and breathed in the aromas of various coffees. As I removed my jacket, my bare arms exposed my flaws.

"That's some serious ink," he said, handing me my coffee.

"Birthmarks," I corrected.

He stared blankly, then shook it off. "Wow, those are so...artistic, precise."

"I get that a lot."

"They're stunning."

"Really, dude?" I laughed. "Stunning isn't what comes to mind. They've branded me as a freak."

His hazel eyes brightened. "You're wrong. And I think it's about time we exchange names." He reached his hand across the table. "My name is Brandon."

I greeted him with my sweetest smile. "Nice to meet you, Brandon. I'm Raven."

"I am sorry if I sound completely insensitive," he pursed his lips, "but I have to ask."

"Just ask me."

"Why are these murders so personal to you?"

My breath trailed off as I slumped against the seat. The guy seated across from me with hazel eyes and dimpled cheeks asked the million-dollar question. Even my parents hadn't figured it out, but a stranger I'd just met did. He'd seen all the witch books I'd chosen, but was it possible for me to look him straight in the eye and reply, *I'm afraid I'm next because I'm a witch?* Could he honestly believe me? Probably not. Should I try? Perhaps. All of this was so overwhelming, and I so badly needed someone to talk to. I shook my hands and exhaled hard. Here goes nothing. "Imagine if you had to share the most important thing in the world with someone but knew they'd never believe you."

An unreadable expression framed his face as he sat still, his eyes on me. "I would try."

My heartbeat quickened as I swallowed the lump in my throat before glancing down at my knees bouncing nervously. I couldn't look him in the eyes as I revealed my most sacred secret. "I have no idea who my biological parents are or where I came from. My adoptive parents found me abandoned at birth in front of a hospital." I glanced up at him and extended my arms. "I don't know why I have these markings. People aren't like me. I'm different."

"Different in what way?" he asked.

I shifted my gaze away as I said, "I have powers, gifts."

His fingers encircled mine, and I met his eyes. "You're a witch, right?"

A meek "Yes," passed my lips.

"You can't use your powers to discover who you are—the marks?"

"No, something is blocking me. Whatever this barrier is, I can't get passed it."

"As someone who has been through some bizarre shit in the past, I believe you." He voiced in an ominous tone. "Now, I need *you* to believe *me.*"

I accepted without hesitation. "Yes, of course."

He paused, and the tension built. "Those girls aren't like you. If there truly was no blood running through their veins, I believe they're vampires."

I fell back against the seat for the second time. Were vampires even real? With a dead serious gaze darkening his eyes, he affirmed wholeheartedly he believed they were. But did I? Could this be the reason he didn't hesitate to believe I was a witch? Was the bizarre period he mentioned related to vampires? It stopped my mind in its tracks. How could it be? They were fictional, or at least in my world they were. "Was that based on personal experience?" I asked.

He smirked. "You don't believe me."

"That's not what I said. I just want something more concrete."

"Like what?"

As I tilted my head, I thought, *What would convince me?* "How about some facts?"

"Facts. Okay," he snapped his fingers. "Got it. There are several levels of vampires: vampire gods, the Old Ones, and the next generation. The Old Ones are a council of vampires who keep all other vampires in line, including the vampire gods. Is this what you're looking for?"

He couldn't have come up with something that detailed and unique on the spot. I leaned forward, narrowing my gaze. "Do you know any vampires?"

"Several."

I burst out laughing when he pulled out his cell phone. "Don't tell me you have vampire selfies?"

"Funny." He dragged his finger across the screen, then flipped it around to reveal a building painted in the purest of black. The only splashes of color came from a gleaming gold door and brilliant red neon letters, floating above the entrance and spelling out Bloodthirst.

"That looks like something straight out of a horror movie. What is it?"

"A vampire bar."

"Not possible."

"Yeah, it's for sure possible. I've been there, and humans go there just to be fed on. The club calls it a vampire kiss."

His expression caught my attention. Neither a glimmer of humor nor doubt crossed his lips. *But a vampire club?* The cold touch of a shiver brushed my skin, and I shook it off. "Have you been fed on?"

"Ha! Not a chance." He lowered his voice. "My situation was different. I went there for help." He wafted a hand over his head. "But that story is for another time. Clearly, Eve can help you discover the truth about your birthmarks and your origins."

"Eve, the person I remind you of, is a vampire?"

"No, sorry, I flipped flopped. Totally different matter. Eve's a witch as well, but more importantly, a psychic. Her clairvoyance is so accurate that it's creepy."

I pursed my lips in thought. Psychics and vampire clubs? What else has he done? Who was this guy? But should I be so judgy? The cray-cray train had also taken me on a ride. They say friendship is everything, but I wouldn't know. I didn't have any. Interacting with others was hard. The closest I got to people was at Cascade Meadows Park. It was my favorite place because of the mature colorful trees, stone walkways, ornate benches, and the variety of people strolling its walkways. As I people watched, I wrote about them in my journal. Like me, he may have been an outsider, not conforming to norms. There was only one way to know for sure if he was telling the truth. I stared at him with my most vulnerable gaze. "Can I meet Eve?"

A smile danced inside his eyes. "Are you up for a road trip? Eve lives in Los Angeles."

My mouth went dry as I thought about what my parents would say. Would they allow me to go off with a stranger? I imagined my dad's brows furrowing as he firmly shook his head no, but I was 19, an adult. Although I had the freedom to make my own decisions, I had to accept Brandon was a complete stranger. A feeling of unease gripped my stomach when I realized that I would have to vet Brandon's trustworthiness before traveling alone with him.

As if reading my mind, he said, "You don't know me. I understand your mistrust, but you can trust me. Hit me up with any questions. What would you like to know?"

"What makes you want to help me?"

He shrugged. "You trusted me with your situation. I have a past too, but a good friend and my sister supported me so I wasn't alone. It doesn't seem like you have anyone."

Despite the sting of his words, they rang true. Although my adoptive parents were there for me, they kept secrets from me. The truth would never come from their lips. This was something I had to do on my own. "You're right." I took a sip of coffee as I watched him from over the rim. "What about your past?"

His shoulders slumped forward as he heaved a deep sigh. "It's complicated."

"I know complicated."

"Not like this, you don't." His jaw clenched. "A dead vampire used my body to store his soul. I hurt people because of him. I craved blood because of him. If it wasn't for a council of vampires, a vampire god, and a good friend, I'd still be stuck with him. Magic kicked his ass to the curb."

My eyelids slid closed, flickered, and shot wide open. "What? Oh my God!"

"There is no doubt that those were the darkest days of my life. As someone who has been labeled as different, I know how it feels. The stares, the name-calling, and the most painful part of all was getting beaten up at school. That wound ended up costing me a trip to the hospital. My mom freaked out and pulled me out of school. After that, she hired Rick, the guy who saved my life."

Words escaped me. Clearly he was telling the truth. Of that I was certain. Yet, how could I be ignorant of vampires? Their existence should have been revealed to me by my magic. A blurry vision of Bloodthirst's gold door entered my mind as I cast a spell to locate the vampire club. The hazy film clinging to my brain gradually lifted. A blast of freezing air met me as I opened the door. The club maintained its fiendish décor with its crimson walls, black-velvet booths, and the stench of human blood, gallons of it. The vampires' eyes, which sparkled like jewels, were an obvious sign of their nature. The pale humans shuffled through the club as fresh blood trickled from tiny holes in their necks. Many others, however, remained lip-locked with vampires all over the place, from booths to walls to the bar. I immediately broke the spell and hugged myself, then brushed the chill off my arms. "I do believe you; I mean vampires being real."

"You look like you saw a ghost," he responded, a wrinkle cutting across his brow.

"You must have suffered so much."

His expression, like that of a lost puppy, melted my heart. His sad smile faded before he waved me off. "Don't feel bad. That happened a couple years ago. I'm fine now."

How could anyone be fine after that? My cheeks burned with shame as I remembered all the times I had felt sorry for myself. His situation had been far worse. My gaze met his, seeing him differently now—vulnerable, broken, real. I was meant to cross paths with this person—was he my kindred spirit? His hazel eyes and dimpled cheeks initially intrigued me, but things had shifted. It was evident that we both experienced abnormalities in our past. The desire to embrace him with all my might shivered down my arms and into my fingertips. I shuddered at the thought. Instead, I softly replied, "I'm glad you're okay now."

He stared at me for a moment as if trying to read my thoughts before cocking his head and blurting, "Remember what I was saying about those girls? That there wasn't blood in their bodies? Well, they fit the vampire description." He flicked his gaze left before returning it to me. "Just not sure why the word witch was carved into their foreheads."

"Can vampires also be witches?"

"I've met some."

With a shrug, I showed my palms. "And?"

"An ancient vampire god fixed me with her magic. Then there's this freaky blonde vampire with the ability to read blood. Another has a connection to the spirit world."

"You've obviously got one up on me. I don't know how to respond to that."

"My point is that you are very different from the dead girls. Maybe you're not in danger."

There were so many questions swirling around in my head that I couldn't keep up. Did Brandon have a point? Was there no threat to me? What types of creatures were these dead girls? How were they selected? What characteristics did they share? Were all of these incidents random, and the killer some sick psycho? Or were they planned, calculated, and a targeted choice of victim? The beginnings of a headache pinched my forehead.

"Perhaps we're looking at this the wrong way," he added, getting my attention. "The words carved into their foreheads might be the killer's signature. Maybe the killer is a witch."

I sucked in a quick breath and covered my mouth. Perhaps he was onto something. Were the girls vampires and the killer was a witch? Could this be a war between vampires and witches? Whatever the case, it was a one-sided battle as only vampires were being slaughtered and put on display. Wouldn't vampires take offense to mockery like that? They'd retaliate if I believed everything I read in books. Ten dead girls now, and nothing but crickets on the killer. Perhaps a witch was too easy a suspect. I mean taking credit for the victim with your signature was pretty bold. Weren't they worried about getting caught or being attacked by vampires? But who was stronger? If such a battle existed, who would win? Vampires are powerful, but witches are clever. Both races could theoretically wipe each other out. Yet, my own burning questions about myself and my parents outweighed those of the dead girls and the killer. "Is that road trip for reals?"

His lips curved in an eager grin. "No doubt. But a plane would be faster."

"If we're going to do this, we need to be able to trust each other. Give me your hands." I offered mine. He didn't hesitate to grasp my hands in his. "I'm going give us a glimpse into our souls.

A pure soul will glisten with light while an impure soul will cloud with darkness."

A frown swallowed up his brow as if he were in pain. His hands trembled against mine before he pulled away. "What if..." he gulped down a breath.

I let my voice soften and I hoped he'd heard the sincerity in my words. "Your soul will glisten, I'm sure of it. You won't be haunted by your past."

"I couldn't go through that again."

I held out my hands. "You won't."

He placed his hands in mine and then held on tight. With my eyes closed, I summoned my power, feeling the soft warmth of magic envelop me. I drifted between the human and witch realms, my breath quickening. The words poured from my tongue with commanding magnitude. "In this place and at this hour, I invoke my ancestor's ancient power. Expose our souls' purest parts or the darkness of our hearts. Open the door, unlock the unknown, and command the unseen to be shown. From life to life, from mind to mind, our souls will now entwine."

As the lines of The Grind blurred, Brandon and I remained, our souls shimmering like sunlight above water. His shoulders trembled with a breath leaving his lips. "There's only light. I'm not gonna lie." He laughed. "I was pretty scared."

"What a beautiful light yours is," I replied before waving my hand in a circle and ending the spell.

"What's next? Los Angeles?"

My parents' objection echoed in the back of my mind. I had to tell them, but how? *Hey, Mom and Dad. I'm heading to Los Angeles with this new guy, but it's all good because I vetted our souls.* Perhaps a lie would work better, or just leave and not say anything. "There's no doubt we're going."

"Sounds like there's a but coming."

"It's my parents."

"I know the feeling."

"Do you live in the dorms or with your family?"

"With my family. You?"

"Same."

"We left Los Angeles because of all that happened." He scrunched his lips as a serious frown gathered between his brows. "My parents won't be happy about me going back there."

"I've never been, but still, the trip won't go over well with my parents. Maybe we shouldn't tell them."

He cut his hand through the air. "Not a good idea. The truth is best even if it's hard to swallow. Me and my sister snuck out of the house when we headed to Bloodthrist. We left a note, but our parents freaked. Thought something had happened to us. They called the cops. When we got home, it wasn't pretty."

The terrified faces of my parents flashed behind my eyes as I let his words sink in. I couldn't put them through that. Them being pissed off at me would be better. "You're right. We should tell them."

He pulled out his phone, then glanced up at me. "Texting Eve. We should make sure she's available. When were you thinking of going?"

"Like yesterday. I've wanted answers my whole life."

"I'll tell her it's urgent and see what she says." He set his phone on the table and glanced at me. "You know, now that I think about it, our parents could give us the old speech: you live in our house, you abide by our rules. Maybe we should tell them at the airport."

Nodding in agreement, I said, "I like that. No confrontation. Just a quick phone call."

A chime interrupted us. He swiped his finger across the screen and smirked. "Eve says come anytime. She will be there."

Chapter 3

As Brandon and I boarded the plane, my parents' gloom-and-doom words of disappointment spun around my head. *What was I thinking? I didn't even know this boy. You're going to be miles from home; what if something happens? This isn't how we raised you.* Part of the blame was on them. Keeping me in the dark was their policy, and because of their secrets, I was flying thousands of miles away with a complete stranger.

His touch on my forearm caught my attention. A sympathetic look tugged at his face. "Are you all right? You haven't said a word since the call with your parents."

A flight attendant pushing a beverage cart interrupted my response. "Good afternoon. I'm Lily. Can I get you two anything to drink or something to snack on? I have water, coffee, tea, orange juice, and soda. For snacks, I have nuts or cookies."

Brandon replied, "Water would be great."

An attractive smile spread across her face as she handed him a bottle of water. She turned to me. "And for you?"

"I'll take some water, too. Thanks."

"Here you are. If you need anything during the flight, just let me know." She continued down the aisle with a smile on her face.

His hand arced in a circle. "You were saying."

I breathed out a heavy sigh as my shoulders slumped. "I got the guilt trip from my parents." My lungs heaved once more. "I just feel sad."

"Oh yeah, my parents thought I was insane going back to where all the drama began."

Having someone I'd just met offer their help and believe in me without knowing me at all made me feel seen and validated. It was a reminder that no matter how small our connection was, there is still hope and kindness in the world. His support gave me the confidence to continue my journey and uncover the secrets that lay ahead. He had no stake in the outcome. I owed him.

"Now it's you who's staring." He smirked and nudged my shoulder.

"You don't even know me, but you didn't hesitate to help me." I laid my hand over my heart. "Am forever grateful."

"Rick was there for me despite not knowing me. Because I was in pain, he did everything he could to help me. It doesn't always take knowing someone to help them."

He seemed to be someone who thought of others before themself. The glimpse I'd gotten of his soul, it shined with beautiful light and empathy, but I lacked faith in people. "It's hard for me to interact with people." I pointed to my birthmarks. "Everyone thinks these are tattoos. When I tell them they're birthmarks, they shy away and avoid me."

"I didn't."

I smiled. "No, you didn't."

"Sometimes friends are overrated. I had several before the whole vampire thing. Now, I just have my sister and Rick."

"How did he save your life? If you don't mind me asking."

His gaze was fixed on me, as if verifying that I was ready for what he was about to say. "Are you sure you want the truth?" he asked with slight caution.

"Yes, of course."

After hesitating, he blurted out, "In order to get it out of me, the vampire's soul had to be transferred to someone else. Rick, being the compassionate human being that he is, offered to help. However, in the process, he became a vampire himself, sacrificing his own humanity for mine."

In disbelief, I stared at Brandon in silence. His words echo in my head, and I couldn't believe what I heard. As his situation sank in, the room blurred around us. "What? He turned into that other vampire?" I asked.

His silence lasted for several seconds before he clarified, "For a while, the other vampire held him hostage, but Rick prevailed."

"Despite being a vampire, you're still friends with him?"

"Well, we don't see each other." He let out a laugh. "You know, the whole vampire versus human thing, but we keep in touch. Eve keeps an eye on him too."

When Eve's name popped into my head, my stomach trembled with excitement. If someone had told me I would be flying to Los Angeles to speak to a psychic, I would have laughed in their face. But there I was, eagerly anticipating the reading and what could be revealed. This was the closest I'd ever come to learning who I was. I'd be happy to receive any information. "My palms are sweating. I can't wait to speak with Eve."

"Despite Eve's reading, there may be unanswered questions. To be safe, I contacted Margarete, a vampire at Bloodthirst. She may be able to help if Eve can't."

My curiosity was piqued when he decided to involve a vampire as a resource. It isn't every day you seek the assistance of a creature that lusts for human blood. "You called a vampire?"

He tilted his head to the side as he replied, "Not exactly." He lowered his voice and added, "Don't freak out, but I have vampire blood inside me. Not from the one who invaded my body, but others who helped me get rid of him. In other words, I can send and receive messages through thought."

"Vampire blood?" I shuddered at the thought. How could he ask me not to freak out? His experiences were not mine. I didn't know anything about that world. Should I be afraid of him? Was he a threat to me? I turned my face away from him and took a deep breath.

"It's okay. Calm down," he whispered.

My birthmarks caught my attention as my hands fell on my lap. Despite telling him I was a witch, that I knew nothing about my past, and that I was gifted with magic, he hadn't freaked out. Could I be overreacting? I glanced at him. His eyes were full of kindness. "I don't know how I feel about all of this."

"It's okay, I totally understand. When we land, I will take you to Eve's and then go back home. I'm stuck with what happened to me, but you don't have to be."

My stomach knotted up in panic, suffocating me with fear of being alone again. His mere presence reassured me. "Don't leave. Please stay."

With conviction and commitment, he said, "I'll stay."

****

In front of Eve's adorable white cottage, our Uber driver dropped us off. Its charming architecture, with its well-trimmed lawn and quaint windows, beckoned us into a psychic's world. The porch was decorated with wind chimes and had a cozy seating area. Brandon hesitated in front of the vibrant red door. After taking a deep breath, he slipped his hands into his faded jeans pockets.

"What's wrong?" I asked.

"The feeling of déjà vu hit me."

"Do you need a moment?" I asked.

"I'm fine," he said, shrugging off his nerves.

As I watched Brandon knock on the door, his trembling hand revealed his inner turmoil. I couldn't help but feel empathy for him. I wanted to reassure him, he wasn't alone in this. As I stood there, I noticed beads of sweat forming on his forehead, betraying his attempt to maintain a composed exterior. It was clear that his past was triggering his anxiety. Although I knew only a portion of his story, I could see how those memories haunted him.

When the door opened, it shattered my thoughts, and Eve caught my attention. Her cherry red lips, which were much more dramatic than mine, lit up in a bright smile. She looked paler to me than I did. Her jet-black hair matched mine perfectly, but mine hung long and straight while hers was short. Her clothes looked like they were straight from the 1970s, unlike my simple black T-shirt tucked into my favorite ripped jeans. I glanced at Brandon, wondering why I reminded him of Eve.

"Brandon, it's good to see you again. You must be Raven. Nice to meet you." She waved us forward. "Come in, come in."

As I entered her front room, a soft, plush rug silenced our footsteps. The walls were adorned with muted artwork that added a sense of sophistication to the room. A sense of unease rose within me, as I realized there was a very high chance I might discover the answers to the questions that had plagued me for so long. "It's nice to meet you too. I hope you can shed some light on my situation."

"Well, let's not wait a second more. My reading room awaits."

We entered Eve's reading room through beaded curtains. The scent of burning incense created a mystic vibe as lava lamps illuminated the bean bag chairs surrounding a round wooden table.

Eve gestured to the chairs. "Please have a seat." Crystals and candles adorned the table, adding a calming effect. "Your blood will stain this cloth. Just a drop guides me through your past, present, and future," she said as she unfolded the white fabric before me.

Brandon cringed. "I forgot about that part."

Putting my hand out, I shrugged. "I'm not squeamish."

"The personal item I ask for is usually jewelry, a keepsake, or an item of clothing, but considering your situation, your birthmarks will carry your unique signature, allowing me to summon your essence."

My jaw dropped as I realized Eve had said birthmarks rather than tattoos. "Can you tell they're birthmarks?" I asked.

Eve's eyes gleamed as she gently traced her fingers over my birthmarks, elaborating on their significance. "It's your witch's mark," she explained.

My birthmarks were always considered tattoos, and people asked if they could photograph them for their tattoo artist. When I explained they were birthmarks, I would get that look that says, "You're a freak," because people seemed to view them negatively. Some even offered to perform rituals or pray for me, thinking I needed protection. Being misunderstood and judged by others was frustrating and confusing. As Eve spoke, she pulled me away from my thoughts.

"Never be ashamed of your symbols of power."

A blanket of warmth covered me, and I smiled. "Thank you, Eve."

"It's my pleasure. Now let's get to work."

With a long needle, she poked my index finger and squeezed out a drop of blood onto the cloth. Warmth and a tingling sensation spread through my fingertip. I rubbed off the sting as soon as she let go. The blood shaped a perfectly round circle, almost hypnotic in its complexity as it weaved its vines into the white fabric.

As she traced my blood's path with her fingertips, she closed her eyes. A wrinkle crossed her forehead as she chanted, "Blood to blood, flesh to flesh, bone to bone, I summon thee. Lead us to what we cannot see." The blood responded, spreading beneath her touch.

A rush of doubt rose in my chest as I watched this mysterious woman meditate on my life force pattern. Could my magic rob Eve of an explanation as it did to me?

She tilted her head as the wrinkle crept deeper into her brow. "There appears to be a powerful magical barrier blocking the source of this blood. The barrier is intricate and well-constructed, clearly the work of a skilled and powerful witch. Another source of magic is also present. Perhaps the barrier is meant to conceal you or protect you from the dark magic. It echoes malevolence and appears to hold hidden intentions."

Every beat of my heart echoed in my ears. I gasped as anxiety gripped my soul firmly, refusing to let go. I shuddered and pressed my arms into my sides. "That's it? There's no more?"

Her jaw tensed, and she breathed exasperatedly. "I can't pass the barrier. I'm sorry."

As I slumped forward, I buried my face in my hands. Would I ever find out who I was?

****

My mind replayed Eve's words as Brandon rattled off some address to the Uber driver. Had someone cast a spell on me? Was

I the barrier? What terrible thing was hidden from me? I feared I would be stuck in this mysterious limbo regarding my birth, my parents, and who I was.

"Don't give up yet," Brandon said, sounding optimistic.

"I know you said not to get my hopes up. But really? She gave me nothing."

A gleam filled his eyes as he focused on me. "Just because Eve failed to deliver doesn't mean we don't have options. I let Margarete know we were coming, and vampires aren't humans, so that barrier might not apply."

"Margarete, is she the one at Bloodthirst?"

Nodding, he said, "She's cool. You'll like her. But Caleb, her partner, is the total opposite."

The implications of his words raced through my mind, and I searched his eyes. "You mean, like dangerous?" I asked.

"No. He's just a sarcastic narcissist."

"So ignore him then?"

He smirked and nudged me. "I'd like to see you try."

"How about a bet?" I asked, sticking out my hand.

As he squeezed my fingers, he smiled. "You're on!"

"Where's Bloodthirst anyway?"

"Castle Beach is three hours away. We've got some time to kill."

The Uber driver caught my attention. Engaging in a get-to-know-you conversation with Brandon would be awkward. I felt self-conscious and hesitant about conversing with him while someone else listened. As the driver continued to look ahead, he maintained the same expression on his face. His car was clean and well-maintained and had a fresh coffee aroma. The quiet hum of the tires on the road created a calming atmosphere, interrupted only by the soft radio buzz.

Brandon picked up on my vibe. "Every conversation doesn't have to be deep. Besides, we already got the heavy stuff out of the way. Why don't we start with likes? I enjoy music, skateboarding, and gaming. You?"

Rolling my eyes, I said, "You're such a guy. I enjoy being one with nature, writing in my journal, and observing people."

A smirk spread across his face. "I never would have thought of you as a tree hugger."

"My favorite thing about trees is the sound they make. Have you ever listened to one?"

His brows furrowed slightly. "I can't say I have."

I rested my hand over my heart as I closed my eyes. "Their leaves sway gently like a romantic whisper in the breeze."

"Wow, that's very poetic. I've never thought about it that way." A genuine smile formed on his lips as he said, "I'm glad we have three hours."

"Me too."

In my first experience outside of Seattle, California stirred my inner tree hugger, as Brandon put it. My gaze drifted out the window and caught the warm sun, the blue ocean horizon, and the mountain peaks dodging the white pillowy clouds that surrounded us. My life had changed drastically in a matter of days, as I had met Brandon, gotten a psychic reading in Los Angeles, and was about to enter the undead world. The images of the dead girls filled my mind. I couldn't escape the feeling that I would become one of them. Was that my destiny? In the event that a higher power led me into the unknown that involved vampires, the truth would become even scarier. Could that be the reason why my adoptive parents kept things from me? Could I be about to open a can of worms? That thought sent a chill slithering down my arms, and I shuddered before brushing off the goose bumps.

Brandon touched my shoulder and soothed my nerves. "I know it's overwhelming," he said. "I've been there before, under different circumstances. We'll figure it out. I promise."

"You can't promise what you don't know." I wasn't being rude or unappreciative, but even with my magic I couldn't predict the outcome. Vampire blood or not, neither could he.

"Maybe not, but I can promise you that I've got your back, just as Rick had mine." He leaned in slightly. "You're not alone in this."

Chapter 4

As we drove through Castle Beach, I couldn't help but gasp at the breathtaking views around us. The rolling hills and lush green landscapes extended as far as the eye could see, creating a picturesque backdrop for the modern majestic castles lining the cliffs. As the sunset sat over the pristine beach below, its golden hues created an unforgettable array of colors shimmering over the water.

The mood changed when the Uber driver turned off the main road and onto Haven Avenue. People walking the streets were creepy as hell under the dim glow of lampposts. Some wore hoodies, some showed a lot of skin, and some stumbled like drunks. My guess was that they were drug dealers, prostitutes, and beggars.

The Uber driver glanced at us in the rearview mirror and said, "1137 Haven Avenue is a few minutes away, but the area seems sketchy. Are you sure this is the address you want?"

"Yes," Brandon said confidently.

A flutter of unease gripped me as I glanced at Brandon. What sort of place was he taking me to?

He nudged my shoulder and smiled. "We'll be ok. Don't worry. The street looks worse than it really is. Besides, we'll be inside the club."

The Uber driver bobbed his head to the left and pointed out, "Might be a while before you get inside. That's a long ass line."

As I peered out of the car window, fear and excitement brushed against my stomach. I couldn't help but feel a sense of foreboding. The ominous presence of Bloodthirst loomed before me. Its dark facade contrasting sharply with the vibrant red neon letters that glowed in the moonlight. The gleaming gold door seemed to taunt me, inviting me to venture into the unknown, but I was determined to resist its intimidation.

Brandon pointed toward the front of the building, "You can let us out there."

As he pulled alongside the club, the wheels bumped up against the curb. He twisted around to face us as he said, "That'll be $452."

Brandon pulled out five hundred-dollar bills from his wallet and handed them to the Uber driver. "Keep the change."

"You two stay safe."

Brandon extended his hand and helped me out of the car. The golden doors held my attention as I stepped onto the sidewalk. He put his hands on my shoulders and forced me to stop. "Don't let that Uber driver's words mess with you. I wouldn't bring you somewhere and not protect you, but they are vampires. You can't let them get inside your head."

"I'm not worried about safety." I pointed at the mob of people. "He's right, though. The line's a mile long. How are we going to get in?"

"Bloodthirst certainly does draw a crowd, but I sent Margarete a message. She's coming out to escort us inside."

I rubbed my hands together as I gazed at the door. "Can't wait."

"This isn't the happiest place on earth." He wagged his finger down the line of people. "They're so amped to get with a vampire that the consequences don't register."

I laughed and nudged him away. "Yeah, right."

"I'm serious." His voice on edge. "People die here. Their bodies are cremated in the back of the club."

I swallowed the taste of bile as my witch brain conjured up the horrid, charred stench of a lifeless body surrounded by crackling flames. How could these vampires just throw a bunch of people into a furnace? It was inhumane, even for a vampire. Did they live, kill, and discard their prey within the same building?

"Another thing, don't stare at them too long. They'll take it as an invitation to feed off you."

Brandon's words interrupted my thoughts and drew my focus toward him. "How can I tell who is human or not?"

"Their eyes set them apart from humans. You'll have no trouble gauging who's who."

"Brandon," a soft female voice called out from behind us.

My pulse quickened as I stared at a tall skinny girl that looked about my age and whose violet-colored eyes captivated me. Was that what Brandon was trying to tell me about how to tell them apart from humans?

She waved us forward, "Come in."

Someone in the crowd yelled, "Hey, what about us? Why do they get to go in?"

Brandon shooed me forward, ignoring the complaint. "Remember, we need her help, not another vampire trying to get your attention. Stay with me."

A vampire pin cushion was not something I wanted to become, but I couldn't promise not to stare. Before today, vampires were fictional characters, not living, breathing creatures operating a nightclub like an amusement park. Nevertheless, I was about to step through the gleaming gold door and into a completely different world.

Bloodthirst's cold, crisp air nipped at my warm skin as I zipped up my jacket and shivered. Was the icy draft caused by the air conditioning or by the large number of cold-blooded vampires? As candles flickered in the darkness, shadows played across crimson walls and black velvet booths. An already unsettling atmosphere was further enhanced by the vampires' intense gazes following every movement in the room.

The stale smell of blood drifted under my nose as Margarete led us to a booth. An image of bloody fangs and drained humans flashed across my mind. My stomach dropped as I tried to push the image out of my head.

"Are you all right?" Brandon asked.

I waved him away. "I'm fine."

Margarete smirked. "You'll get used to the smell."

Brandon glanced at his cell when it suddenly rang. His lips tightened as he frowned. "Why is Eve calling me? Hello? You're not making any sense. Slow down. Who's there with you?" He ran his hand through his hair. "Eve, are you there? Eve?" His voice rose as he repeated, "Eve!" After a few moments, he looked at us and said, "The call dropped."

"Call her back," Margarete urged.

Brandon tapped his cell and then pressed it against his ear. "It's going to voicemail."

"Is there something wrong?" I asked.

He stared at me but didn't say anything.

Margarete brushed her dark hair away from her face as she narrowed her gaze at Brandon. "I've already sent Caleb to Eve's. You should call 911."

"What's going on?" I asked again, my voice rising in concern.

As soon as Brandon tapped his phone, he reached 911. "I think my friend's in trouble. I got a call from her and heard this weird cackling sound in the background and then the call dropped. I tried to call her back but it went to voicemail. Her name is Eve. Her last name? Sorry, I don't know it. Yes, I have her address. It's 11479 Bay Passage, Los Angeles. Can I stay on the line until the police arrive? Okay, thanks."

Brandon pacing back and forth as he waited on the phone made me dizzy. How long had he been waiting: five, ten minutes? If you dial 911 for an emergency, shouldn't they respond immediately? I felt clammy sweat cling to my palms as I stared at Brandon's grimace and Margarete's cool and collected expression. As usual, I was kept in the dark. What were they hiding from me? Was Eve okay? Had someone broken in? What else had she said to Brandon? Was she in danger?

Brandon let out a gasp. "Is Eve okay? You're unable to share that information with me? Okay, I see. Is there a way I can find out? A member of the family? As I mentioned, I am merely a friend. Okay, thanks." His posture sagged as he shoved his cell back into his jeans pocket. A shake of his head followed. "They won't tell me anything."

I threw up my hands. "I'm standing right here. I can hear you. Will one of you please tell me what's going on?"

Margarete nudged Brandon. "Tell her. She needs to know."

He lowered his head to meet my eye level, his voice losing its luster as he spoke. "Eve said, 'Dark magic has risen. Battles will be lost. You must save her.'" Brandon paused, gazing painfully at the ground. "I heard laughter, high-pitched crazy laughter, and then Eve said, 'What belongs to me won't be yours. I will never betray her.' A loud crack came through the phone, ending the call." He pulled away and looked at Margarete as if she held the answers.

I dissected Eve's words. Risen? Battles? Won't be yours? Brandon was right. It made no sense at all. "What does that mean?"

Brandon shrugged. "I don't know."

"Caleb will have more information," Margarete assured. "He'll be here soon."

"He's already on his way back? We took three hours to get there."

"You silly child. Vampires fly at the speed of light."

"Child?" I huffed. "I'm 19." I eyed her up and down. "And from the looks of it, you're the same age as me."

"I was 17 years old when I became a vampire. That was 127 years ago."

A weak, "I'm sorry," was all I could muster as I gawked at her. The realization hit me like a blow to the chest—to never age, to always be physically the same, but to continuously evolve emotionally and intellectually. There was something tantalizing about it, leaving me both fascinated and scared.

Her pearly white fangs gleamed as she grinned. "Apologies aren't necessary. I'm quite pleased with myself now."

A whoosh of air lifted my hair as the most handsome man I'd ever seen swept past me. Glossy, long auburn hair, sparkling hazel eyes, and scarlet lips. Panic surged through me as my eyes landed on Eve, her limp body dangling in his grasp. Her lifeless eyes stared into space, unblinking and empty, her lips slightly parted as if still gasping for air. Fearing she was dead, I felt my own blood draining from my face.

Margarete fixed her gaze on Eve and demanded, "Caleb, what happened?"

"Oh...God...is...she...dead?" Brandon spluttered his words, his face growing whiter and whiter.

"No," Caleb confirmed, "but there isn't time to explain. We need to leave. Now!" His hazel eyes caught mine before landing on Margarete. "Can you take Brandon and the girl?"

"Where?"

"The Council's Haven."

She pressed her lips into a thin line as she raised a single eyebrow. Her body language clearly expressed her disagreement. What made her react so strongly to the Council's Haven?

"The clock is ticking, Margarete," Caleb urged. "Share your blood, and let's get skyrocketing."

Margarete narrowed her eyes and did nothing to comply with his demands. Several seconds later, she turned to Brandon, dug her fangs into her wrist and offered it to him. "Drink."

Brandon's voice rose as he refused her blood and blurted, "Tell me what happened at Eve's."

Caleb kept his cool as he pushed Brandon toward Margarete. "Like I said, no time. Now, drink."

Caleb's orders weren't disobeyed a second time as Brandon inched closer to Margarete, with his mouth wide open. Watching her blood drip into his mouth turned my stomach and I gagged on bile. When she turned to me, my heart pounded against my rib cage. "You want me to drink your blood? No."

"You must drink," she insisted. "We travel fast, too fast for a human. Your life depends on my blood." She raised her bloody wrist. "Drink."

I shook my head and clamped my mouth shut.

Caleb shouted, "Drink the blood for God's sake!"

Brandon squeezed my hand and reassured me, "I promise, Raven, it won't hurt or change you. It's to protect you."

I shut my eyes before opening my mouth and accepting her blood. The taste of salt and copper rolled over my tongue and down my throat. Margarete wrapped her arm around my waist and pulled me into her side before latching onto Brandon with her other arm. She propelled us forward with insane speed. My head jerked backward. Everything was a blur, but as the cool night air nipped at my skin, I knew we'd exited Bloodthirst.

Wind ripped through my flesh and robbed me of heat. I cried out and clung to her, terrified of being torn apart by the relentless wind. Tears streamed down my face as the deafening gusts whipped around me and pummeled my eardrums.

I could feel Margarete's warm breath against my ear as she whispered, "Just hold on, we're almost there."

Thoughts raced through my mind, wondering if we would ever reach safety and survive this harrowing journey. As I grasped onto her words like a life preserver, a glimmer of hope flickered before my world went black.

Chapter 5

Upon opening my eyes, I saw several regal high-back chairs arranged around a long marble table. I sat facing the table in a similar chair. To the right of the table, Margarete and Caleb were deep in conversation with a man and a woman dressed in lavish cloaks. The fact that their skin was pale and their eyes were jewel-like captivated me, but their cloaks scared me the most, giving me the impression that we had traveled back in time. However, I knew that was impossible, but where was I?

My warm skin shuddered in the chill of uncertainty. Where was Brandon? He was my comfort zone—the only person I knew on this wild ride. As I peeked around the side of the chair, he sat slumped in a chair beside me, his eyelashes fluttering. "Brandon," I whispered to avoid drawing attention from the strangers across the room.

He sat straight up, his gaze settling on me. I must have looked like I was in a state of terror as he grabbed my hand and assured, "Don't be scared. We're safe with these vampires. Trust me, I know." He pointed at a male with long blonde hair. "That's Kohath, head of the Council and Caleb's maker. Athaliah, the blonde next to Kohath, is one of his Council members and has the ability to read blood."

Seeing the power emanating from the two of them sent alarms ringing in my head. The desire to learn about my birthright faded away. I hugged my arms, mimicking my adoptive parents' warmth as I said to Brandon, "At the moment, I don't feel safe."

Apparently, he didn't hear me. His wide eyes darted around the room as he jumped from the chair and charged at Caleb. He clenched his hands and demanded, "Where's Eve?"

Caleb pushed his hands downward. "Stabilize, Cass. It would have been pointless for me to rescue her if I was just going to turn around and drain her."

"Our doctors are currently examining her. She has been in and out of consciousness, and is extremely weak, but rest assured, she will survive," Kohath said to Brandon.

Brandon released a loud breath. "Thank God."

"In spite of these trying circumstances, I am glad to see you, son."

"Good to see you too, Kohath. I brought someone along with me." Brandon waved me over. "This is Raven."

As all eyes were on me. My heart raced and my hands trembled. I wanted to impress, not look frightened, stumble over my words, or fall short of expectations.

Brandon bobbed his head in their direction. "Raven, this is Kohath and Athaliah."

Kohath cupped my hands in his, letting me feel warm skin such as a human instead of the dead, cold flesh of a vampire. I flinched at the reality, but quickly composed myself. I shook his hand. "Hello."

The thick eyebrows that framed his olive-colored eyes drew together as he smiled. "Dear child, we welcome you to our haven. You will be protected here."

I cocked my head and questioned, "Protected from what?"

Brandon's expression mirrored my confusion. "Yes, why does she need protection?"

"While you two were sleeping off the vampire buzz," Caleb interrupted, "I took the opportunity to update Kohath and Athaliah. Eve was attacked by some crazy witch demanding details about you." He pointed at me.

"Me?"

"Yes, you. When I got there, the witch was screaming something about the girl who had come with the boy. Eve was slumped over in her chair and barely hanging on, so I grabbed her and rushed out." A stern stare crossed Caleb's face as he folded his arms. "How did that witch know you'd been there, and why is she so hell-bent on finding you?" he asked.

"I don't know." I answered lamely, but the truth was the truth. "I told my parents I was going to Los Angeles. I didn't mention Eve at all."

"I did," Brandon admitted. "My parents knew I was planning on seeing Eve, but they wouldn't..." A look of pain gripped Brandon's face as he raked his hands through his hair. "Oh God. I have to call them." He hurried off to the other side of the room. I remained fixated on him even as he turned away for privacy. He stood motionless for a long moment before exhaling a deep breath and speaking into his phone.

Shortly afterward, he rejoined us. "They're fine, but still mad at me."

Brandon's remark about the safely of his parents seemed irrelevant to Caleb. He had not taken his eyes off me. "Why you?" he asked again. "This witch was extremely powerful, so much so that she was draining Eve in order to gain information about you. What makes you so intriguing? It seems you're at best a novice witch, who is incapable of mastering a spell to unlock your own birthrights. What does this witch want with you?"

As Brandon said, I couldn't ignore him, and his constant questions were exhausting. Tension grew throughout the room as everyone awaited my response. I knew I had to say something, anything, to get him to stop. My frustration got the better of me, and I sarcastically replied, "Your guess is as good as mine."

"Interesting." He tapped his chin. "But the question still requires an answer."

Kohath echoed that. "Excellent point."

"You're just badgering her," Margarete scolded.

With affection, Caleb said, "Humor me, love."

As if she had heard that line a thousand times before, she waved him away.

Athaliah stepped forward, raising her voice as she proclaimed, "She bears the mark of a witch. Show us your arms."

The vampire's jewel-like eyes remained fixed on my jacket, eagerly waiting for me to remove it. After releasing a nervous breath, I tossed it on the chair, then held out my arms. I knew I had no choice but to obey them, but Eve's words "Never be ashamed of them" filled me with strength.

"Behold!" Athaliah exclaimed with a wave of her hand toward me as if I were a sculpture she had created.

Caleb jerked his head back and lowered his gaze. "I didn't see that coming." He chuckled. "Quite impressive!"

Margarete's eyes widened as she ran her finger along the length of my arm. "I have never seen anything like that." She glanced over at Caleb. "It's so precise, like a work of art."

Kohath leaned forward and examined them carefully. His gaze flickered upward as he met my eyes. "I saw similar symbols on ancient temple walls long before vampirism emerged. They symbolized significant power. Although *you* do not possess this power, it seems strange as to why you would bear such marks."

"The blood she sheds will reveal the truth," Athaliah said curtly.

I clutched my throat, feeling the imaginary fangs piercing my skin and the pain radiating through my body. My voice trembled as I demanded an explanation, desperate to understand the ominous meaning of the statement. "What does that mean exactly?"

"The blood in your body can be read in two ways: with my fangs or with my dagger." Her wild gaze shot to my neck. As she met my eyes, her expression softened. "Which do you prefer?"

"Are there any other options to my blood?" I pleaded in desperation, my pulse quickening. Nobody was robbing me of my blood. Wouldn't a magic spell accomplish what they needed without causing me such distress?

Athaliah scowled at me. Evidently casting doubt on her abilities wasn't cool with her.

"Isis might be able to help." Brandon offered up. "I reached out to her but didn't hear back."

"Osiris and Isis are abroad, visiting Horus," Kohath explained. "They are unlikely to return for several months."

"Stop wasting time. We're in this situation because of you," Caleb preached as he nudged me toward Athaliah. "Reading your blood is the fastest way we resolve this mess."

"Don't blame her," Brandon argued. "She's in the dark like the rest of us."

Caleb's gaze widened as it traveled between Brandon and me. "Clearly, she's bedazzled you. Do you know for certain that she is in the dark?"

"I'm trying to help her. That's what humans do."

"Ha!"

Margarete sneered at Caleb before stepping between them. Caleb flopped into a chair and threw up his hands. She ignored his theatrics and turned to me. "I understand your resistance. However, we are offering a viable solution. I would accept it."

As much as I didn't want to give in, it was probably the safer option. Taking on such a powerful vampire might have dire consequences, so I bravely took the option of the dagger. "No fangs."

"I will retrieve my dagger and goblet." Athaliah's eyes brimmed with excitement as she nodded to her companions and quietly left the room.

"I think I'm gonna throw up," I whispered to Brandon.

"I'll be right beside you. It'll only take a few seconds."

"Will it hurt?"

As he rubbed the center of his palm, he admitted. "I'm not gonna lie. It's not pleasant."

It meant a lot to me that Brandon showed such concern and commitment to my situation despite the fact that I knew almost nothing about him. We had shared an immediate connection, and I had clear reasons for trusting Brandon. However, I did not know why he trusted me. Caleb's comment popped into my head, so I had to ask. "I know you said you were in this because of what happened to you. But Caleb—"

"Caleb loves to get a rise out of people. Don't let him get to you." He held my hands tightly. "I believe everything happens for a reason. We bumped into each other for a reason, not because I had a hidden agenda."

"Okay."

"Are we good?"

"We're good."

The whoosh of the door caught my attention as Athaliah entered with a tray containing an ancient golden goblet and a sterling dagger. She set the tray carefully on the table in front of an empty chair. As she reached for her silver dagger, it caught the light and a shimmer rippled across the room.

"Remember, I'll be right there with you," Brandon whispered into my ear before taking my hand and leading me toward the table.

Upon her signal to sit down, I cautiously lowered myself into the chair, gazing at the dagger before me. Its blade carried intricate patterns etched in its surface that radiated power and danger. An eerie sense of dread swept over me. I was stuck in an unfamiliar place, with vampires no less. Running seemed pointless, but I desperately wanted to escape. I was in over my head. I should've listened to my parents. I'd be home right now, sound asleep in my bed instead of being trapped in this horrible nightmare. There was one upside to all of this—Athaliah might uncover my origins if she could break through the barrier that I and Eve could not.

Athaliah's expression grew cold as she pressed her blade against my skin. The sting of my flesh being slit open made my muscles tense, and I cried out. My body trembled, and I screamed again. I was a wimp, incapable of handling pain. However, vampires saw fear as weakness, so I had to show courage, not fear, if I wanted to survive.

As Athaliah removed the dagger and placed my hand over the top of the goblet, I felt my palm tingle with a magnetic pull. As soon as my next breath came, I believed the goblet had some mystical power which called upon my blood. My blood flowed into the goblet as it left me.

Using one of her fangs, Ataliah punctured her finger and applied blood to my open wound. As she let go, invisible sutures pulled my skin taut. I examined my hand and blinked. The damage from her dagger left no traces on my skin.

Her eyes glazed over as she swallowed my blood, and then her eyelids fluttered closed, immersed in the spell of my blood. A few minutes passed before she spoke. "A veil covers the origins of this blood, but its power cannot compare with mine. I have found the father."

My heart thumped inside my chest as I leaned closer, eager to hear the revelation. The suspense suffocated me, and I couldn't contain the mix of anticipation and fear bubbling inside me. Every fiber of my being yearned for clarity, to find out who this mystery person was. I wanted to know if he was truly my father and what he meant to my life.

In an instant, Kohath reached Athaliah's side and laid his hand on her shoulder. "His daughter is entitled to an explanation from him. Athaliah, do you have a location?" He glanced over his shoulder at Caleb, sharing an unspoken message. Caleb nodded. "Caleb will bring him here."

My stomach clenched as an emotional roller coaster of anticipation, curiosity, and vulnerability swept through me. As much as I dreaded and longed for this meeting, I wondered whether he would recognize me, if the meeting would answer my questions or raise new ones. But what if he wasn't interested in being part of my life, or worse, hurtful or harmful?

"Caleb's attempt to locate him might be unsuccessful due to his masked presence," Athaliah explained. "I must accompany Caleb to collect the father."

"Oh, ye of little faith," Caleb scornfully taunted, "I assure you I can be quite resourceful."

Athaliah looked at Kohath.

"I take heed of your warning, Athaliah," Kohath assured her. "Finish your reading and then go with Caleb to collect her father."

Caleb folded his arms and mumbled something to Margarete. He was clearly unhappy. She wrapped her arm around him and whispered something back. If I were him, I wouldn't have wanted a babysitter either. But this wasn't about him. This was about my father and me.

As Athaliah became consumed by her blood ritual, her eyes grew wild and unfocused as her hands carefully traced intricate patterns in the air. She began to mutter words under her breath before snapping her head upright.

"Athaliah, what is it?" Kohath inquired, his voice heightened.

"Her blood..." She paused as her intense expression deepened. "I see darkness, betrayal, and punishment."

Her voice echoed in my mind, each word cutting like a knife. Moments later, the room seemed to close in around me. My thoughts raced, trying to process the information. Questions and fears swirled through my brain. How would I cope if this were true?

"It'll be all right," Brandon assured as he squeezed my hand. "We'll figure it out."

"I'm not a terrible person." I blurted out in a shrill voice. "I haven't betrayed anyone. Why would I be punished? I don't understand what you're saying."

"Silence!" Athaliah shouted. "The blood is still speaking to me."

I held back a whimper. Bawling wasn't going to solve any-thing, but I just couldn't stand there while she doled out informa-tion piece by piece. "Then tell us what it's saying!"

"Be patient, I will reveal the information as it comes to me." She stopped and cocked her head as if listening to someone. "You were not born from your biological mother. Your ancient ancestors chose a surrogate host whose betrayal led to their punishment."

I glanced at the others, trying to gauge their reactions. Their expressions showed a mix of confusion and frustration, suggest-ing that they were just as puzzled as I was. Several members raised their eyebrows, acknowledging the need for clarification. Margarete was the first to ask, "Who is her mother?"

"The key to unlocking this mystery lies in the ancient ances-tors' magical power. Her blood, however, has revealed the surro-gate host and her dark magic."

Margarete flinched. "Why choose a host that dwells in a world of dark magic?"

"The darkness overtook the host only after the child was born," Athaliah explained.

My own life unfolded before my eyes. I knew nothing about my birth, including the identity of my mother. I wondered if the marks on my arms held any clues about the surrogate and dark magic. Did I have dark magic in me? None of it made sense.

"How dark is this little host now?" Caleb sounded off in his annoying tone.

"It appears that the host has been consuming witches' blood and souls in order to gain their power," Athaliah calmly replied. "By now, I would imagine she's quite powerful and extremely dark."

As the images of the dead girls crashed into my brain, the pieces fell into place like a puzzle. The weight of the truth crushed me as I realized my mother was the witch killer. As I stood up, I cried out, "My mother murdered those girls. "

"Not your mother, but the host," Athaliah corrected. "By absorbing their power, she believes she can defeat you. In her eyes, the power you possess is rightfully hers, and it's what she craves. Her relentless pursuit of control will lead her here."

With my arms pinned against my stomach, I took a deep, painful breath. Because of this sick person, I unknowingly contributed to the deaths of those girls. "But I'm not powerful," I cried and pointed at Caleb. "As he said, I couldn't even master a spell."

Caleb cocked his head and wagged his finger at me. "I actually said you were incapable of mastering a spell to unlock your own birthrights."

I waved him away. "Whatever, same thing."

"Contrary to what you say, I beg to differ."

I let out an exaggerated groan. "You're so annoying."

"Why, thank you."

"It's not a compliment."

Athaliah turned my head toward her. "Ignore him. We have more important things at hand." She faced the others. "The host is coming. We must prepare."

Kohath scoffed. "The Council will never be challenged by a fool."

"It is therefore wise to consider her a fool as she is coming with a vengeance."

Kohath raised his brows. "Does she not fear such a battle?"

"The risks of war are meaningless to her if she conquers the power she desires," Athaliah stated, and not in her usual composed manner.

Kohath's gaze centered on me, and then narrowed. "You truly have no knowledge of this host?"

"No, I swear."

"I can vouch for her," Brandon said, standing beside me.

Caleb waved him away. "Bedazzled, as I said before."

"Raven's blood is our proof," Athaliah affirmed before approaching Kohath. "Contact the Ten, specifically Isis. We can defeat the witch if we combine our forces."

When I looked around the room, I felt helpless and disoriented. Imposing vampire gods, the Council, and dark magic made it impossible for me to breathe. The surrogate host only added to the confusion. As numbness spread throughout my brain, I lost focus and gripped the armrest before falling back into the seat. The room faded into a blur, and the voices around me became distant echoes. My head rocked backward, and my eyelids fluttered shut as the cold, clammy grip of unconsciousness took over.

I opened my eyes to find myself alone in the room. Where was everyone? What the hell was going on? It seemed odd that they would just leave me there. Just outside the chamber door, footsteps echoed in the hallway, and a sense of dread swept through me. As I slowly rose, I searched for anything I could use to protect myself. The goblet caught my eye, and I grabbed it off the table and raised it over my head.

Brandon entered the room and his gaze landed on me with the goblet over my head, ready to strike. He ducked and said, "You're not going to hit me with that thing, are you?"

I quickly lowered my arms and breathed a sigh of relief. "Where did everyone go? What happened?"

He smirked and approached me. "I'll take that as a no. You passed out."

My head twisted in confusion as I stared at him. "So you just left me?"

"Oh no, of course not." He seemed just as surprised as I was. "Once you regained consciousness, Kohath's staff prepared some food for us, but you refused to leave this room and asked me to bring it to you."

"I don't see any food here."

"I was coming back to let you know it's almost ready."

A blurry image appeared in the doorway, hovering about a foot above the floor. I squinted, trying to make what it was. "Do you see that?" I whispered.

A woman's voice hissed inside my ear, "Surrender what is mine or he will certainly breathe his last breath." The image in the doorway spiraled forward, knocking chairs out of its path. Its spider-like arms sprang out and engulfed Brandon, encasing him inside its blurred vortex. When he screamed, it pierced my soul and chilled me to the bone. My heart raced as I ran after him, shouting out his name, "Brandon!"

A hand gripped my shoulder as a muffled voice filled my head. "I'm right here. Raven, wake up."

My eyes flew open as Brandon's voice freed me from my nightmare. An old-fashioned bedroom with two twin beds, a huge dresser, and a small seating area surrounded me. I was lying on one of the beds, and Brandon was sitting next to me. Lines of concern were etched into his forehead, and alarm glowed in his eyes. As I gazed at him, relief once again flooded my body. He was safe and sound. "Thank God you're okay," I murmured as I hugged him tight.

He stroked my hair and said, "Raven, it was just a dream. It's okay. I'm fine."

Being fully awake, I wondered if it had been a dream or was it a vision of what's to come? If that was a glimpse into the future, no one around me was safe. That insane person would make sure of that.

Chapter 6

As in my dream or vision, Kohath's staff prepared a meal for Brandon and me. While I headed back to the room, Brandon stayed in the kitchen, chatting with the chefs.

In the privacy of the room, I sent my adoptive parents a single text, "I am fine, but I won't be home for a few days." I turned off my phone immediately afterward. I wasn't up for the freakout they would unleash, and if they knew what I was knee deep in, or that I was about to meet my biological father, they'd go ballistic. The whirlwind of information over the last few days left me feeling numb, exhausted, and overwhelmed, and I hadn't a clue what to do, so dealing with my parents just seemed impossible right now.

A soft tap on the door caught my attention. As I opened it, I stared into the jewel-like eyes of a fair-skinned woman with platinum blonde hair. At once, I ducked behind the door as a vampire alert went off inside my head.

Her hand hovered over her heart as she introduced herself. "I'm Teresa. You have been summoned to the Council's chambers, and I am to escort you."

My eyes stayed fixed on her. What if this was just a trick to lure me to some secluded place and drain me of blood? I didn't budge. How could I know if she was telling the truth?

Her lips spread into a phony grin. "Do not be afraid of me. I am not interested in your blood. The Haven is a sanctuary for vampires, and we are bound by its rules to reside here. My task is only to bring you to the Council."

With my hand still gripping the doorframe, I glanced into the hallway, looking both right and left. There was nobody there. I met her eyes. "Where is Brandon?"

"He and the others are already there. You are the only one not present."

"Others?"

"The Council, Caleb, Margarete, and a human man are awaiting your arrival."

Adrenaline surged through my veins as I realized that "human man" could only mean one thing: my father was here. Any concerns about my safety around Teresa vanished, and all I could think about was confronting my father. "Take me there," I demanded.

Her path led me through many hallways and finally into a dark corridor. Each doorway was adorned with ivory statues carved in the form of mythical gods. Teresa stared straight ahead, ignoring their superior expressions while I shivered and hugged my arms.

Two hanging lanterns lit up the end of the corridor, revealing a solid black door with silver trimming. My breath quickened, mimicking my anxious heartbeat. On the other side sat my father. My eyes immediately focused on the room as she opened the door and motioned for me to enter.

As I took my seat next to Brandon, I passed twelve flawless beings sitting around the marble table. The Council's jewel-like eyes swept over me, before they turned their attention to a pale-skinned man with black spikey hair. His graphic T-shirt, faded jeans, and leather high-top sneakers indicated he was not much older than me. I could not possibly be this man's daughter.

It was Athaliah who approached the man in front of her fellow comrades. "He is not a witch, nor human as I had originally read from Raven's blood. He is one of us, a vampire. It is impossible for him to have fathered a child." She pointed at me as she whipped her head toward him. "Explain your relationship with her."

A chuckle escaped his lips as he shrugged. "*He* has a name. It's Nico. Like I said when you and your goon friends kidnapped me, I don't know her."

Athaliah glanced at me and commanded, "Let him see your marks."

With a huff, I threw my jacket on the chair where it would remain for the foreseeable future. Taking the damn thing off all the time was getting old.

Nico scooted to the edge of his seat, blinked, and narrowed his gaze on me as he whispered, "It's you." He laughed, but it was tinged with anxiety. "I never expected to see you again."

"Then you do know her?" Kohath asked.

Nodding slightly, Nico said, "But I'm not her father."

"She carries your blood. Tell us how that is possible?" Athaliah demanded.

A downturned expression covered his face. "I saved her from her psycho mother."

As I shifted in my seat, I hugged my body to protect myself from whatever he would say next. Brandon leaned closer to me and grabbed my hand, and I clung to his.

"Don't judge, but an abandoned church is where I go to gather my thoughts. On that particular night, I found this extremely pregnant girl by the altar. She was doubled over and in labor, so no time to get her to a hospital. I went to help her and I could see the umbilical cord was wrapped around the baby's neck."

Athaliah looked Nico up and down. "How would you know such a thing?"

"I was a paramedic. Being a vampire ended that career. Too much blood and all." One glare from Athaliah and he switched back to the story of my mother. "I told her to stop pushing so I could unwrap the cord. From there, she pushed like twice and then this little baby girl was laying in my arms, crying her first cry."

Athaliah pursed her lips as she grilled him with questions. "What happened to the mother? Where is she now? Did you kill her?"

"Do you want to hear my story or not?"

She gestured a forward motion with her hand. "Continue."

"The girl's face lit up as she gazed at the birthmarks covering her baby's arms. She grabbed the baby from me, laughing this crazy laugh, and chanting, 'The power will be mine'."

As Nico spoke about my birth, an unsettling heaviness spread across my chest. The fact that she'd given birth alone and in the presence of a vampire didn't seem significant to her. My birthmarks seemed to mattered more. Although I was desperate to know the truth, hearing the story of my birth left me feeling more broken and isolated.

"Her blue eyes grew dark, almost black, as she stared at her baby. Then that crazy freak bit her own child and sucked on her blood. The mother was no vampire either."

I shuddered as a lump of fear rose in my throat. The idea of my own mother stealing my blood and using it for her own gain horrified me. I couldn't comprehend how a mother could be so detached from her own child.

Nico's eyebrows arched into a thoughtful expression as he said, "I'm sorry you have to hear this."

Kohath stood up and loomed over Nico. "And you just stood there and watched?"

He shooed Kohath away. "No, of course not. I'm not a baby killer. I grabbed the baby and healed her with my blood."

"That explains why your blood is inside her," Athaliah pointed out.

My whimper echoed in my ears as I covered my face with my hands. What was the significance of her wanting my blood? Why would she become pregnant and carry me for nine months, only to kill me? In my mind, Athaliah's words resurfaced, *that person was never your mother. She is just a host.* Had my real mother discovered what the freak was up to and tried to stop her, only to be killed by her? Had she died protecting me?

"I'm here for you, Raven," Brandon said, moving his chair even closer to me. "You don't have to go through this alone."

I fixed my eyes on him before scanning every face in the room. Dismay obscured their expressions, including Caleb's, but it didn't matter if they sympathized with me. I shook my head hard, freeing my mind of the damaging words. It would not do me any good to continue to hear how I did not matter and that I was a pawn in her grab for power. I rose to my feet and pointed at Nico. "He isn't my father and knows nothing about my real mother. Being here has only caused me more suffering, more pain. I want to go home."

Caleb stood across the room a minute ago, but now he was inches from me. His narrowed gaze reeked of impatience as it burned into my flesh. "It's too late to declare game over. It's not just about you anymore." He jabbed a finger at his chest. "When you stepped into Bloodthrist, you involved me, Margarete, the Council, and Eve, who nearly lost her life."

My eyes brimmed with tears as I balled my fists. I knew he would mock me for crying. It took all my strength to shove the pain deep down inside me and keep my head high. "I came here for answers, for help." My gaze drifted to Nico. "He is a sorry excuse for either."

"Hey now. I am a victim too," Nico pointed out.

Everyone's attention was caught by the whoosh of the door opening, followed by wheels rubbing against the stone floor. An elderly woman wheeled Eve into the room. Eve's pale, haggard appearance made me sick to my stomach. A bag of ruby-red blood hung above the wheelchair and streamed through clear tubing into Eve's arm. Despite the blood, none of the vampires seemed affected.

"I'm so sorry to interrupt, but after she woke, we were unable to calm her. She continued to rattle on about Raven and Brandon," the woman explained to the Council.

After catching sight of Eve, Brandon rushed to greet her. "I'm so glad that you're okay," he said as he hugged her.

Reaching for his arm, her whole body trembled. "I have information I must share." She glanced at me. "Your marks contain a hidden message—a code that unlocks your power."

Caleb blocked my path before I could even step toward Eve. "Hold up, Sparky." He turned away from me and deliberately lowered his head to stare at Eve. "What do you mean by this?"

"As this witch drained me, our blood mixed. I felt her emotions, read her thoughts, viewed her past. She's terrified Raven will unlock the code and destroy her."

"Of course." Athaliah nodded animatedly. "The mixing of blood opened a window into her soul."

The tone of Caleb's voice turned serious as he asked, "Did this glimpse show you anything else?"

"Like how we obtain the code?" Margarete added.

As sweat beads lined Eve's forehead, she struggled to brush them away. "S-she does n-not know the c-code," Eve answered, her voice shaky and weak.

"She needs to return to her room as soon as possible," the woman said after wiping Eve's forehead.

"Absolutely, Edith, and she will. Just a few more questions," Kohath replied, before turning to Eve and wondering, "Why does she think that a code exists?"

"She pledged to serve as the ancestor's host, but greed for power consumed her." Eve's eyelids fluttered and her voice struggled. "She...believed she could...outsmart the ancestors and consume the baby's power. For her betrayal, they imprisoned...her in a magical tomb and revealed the...hidden code within Raven's birthmarks."

"A tomb?" Margarete gasped.

Was I just a vessel of power? A prize to be fought over? Something to be thrown away like garbage? Nico's voice shattered my crestfallen thoughts, and his words brought me back to reality.

"I witnessed their wrath and this so-called tomb." He glanced at me and his lips formed the word "sorry" before continuing. "The ground rumbled and two loud booms echoed beneath its surface as thick fog rose from the floorboards. It spurted into the air and flew at her. I didn't wait around to find out what happened next. I took the baby and bolted."

Kohath's brow wrinkled as he directed his question to Eve. "I assume she was never meant to be freed. How did she escape?"

"As the tomb held her prisoner, she called out to the gods of dark magic. For nineteen years, she cast thousands of spells against the tomb's walls until finally they crumbled away, freeing her."

"I'm 19," I said.

"And that's when the murders began," Brandon added.

Eve's hands fell limp in her lap and she sagged in the chair, muttering, "As I-I saiddd…"

Edith grabbed the wheelchair and angled the chair toward the door. "I'm taking her back to her room."

"Wait," Eve blurted, holding Edith back. "The witch now seeks revenge, not just power. She murdered those witches, robbing them of blood and magic to gain power. If we cannot unlock the code, she will kill Raven."

A chorus of retorts erupted in the room. Caleb's voice being the loudest as he argued, "That's a bit harsh."

I fell backward into my seat and I closed my eyes. The buzz of angry sentiments did not hold my attention. I couldn't concentrate on meaningless words—only one—kill. The ancestors created a child, and I was that child—a product of their magic, born with a particular purpose unknown to me. It appeared that the host had the advantage of this knowledge and she wanted me dead because of it. The steady thump-thump…thump-thump…thump-thump of my heartbeat brought a calmness to my body and quieted my thoughts but did not ease the growing fear that I was being hunted.

Brandon nudged my shoulder and whispered, "Open your eyes, Raven. Isis and Osiris, aka Cleopatra and Jim Morrison, just walked into the room."

I jerked my head toward him. "What?"

He pointed across the room. "Look."

A regal aura enveloped Kohath and his crew, but the two vampires who entered were statuesque beyond compare. Their eyes glowed with a supernatural light and their skin was pale, like the moonlight washing over them. The male wore a distressed crossbones T-shirt, jeans, and high-top sneakers, starkly different from female's ruched crop top, straight-leg trousers, and Egyptian sandals. When I glanced at my ripped jeans and simple black T-shirt, I felt extremely ordinary.

They moved with an air of power and authority that commanded respect, and all those present should bow in reverence. As they walked toward the Council's table, their feet glided across the floor like they had never touched it. Kohath kissed the female on each gorgeous cheek before shaking the male's hand.

Her gray eyes narrowed, then widened, and within one blink she stood in front of me whispering, "I haven't seen these since…"

"Isis, what is it? What's wrong?" the Jim Morrison doppelganger, as Brandon called him, asked, wrapping his arm around her.

She pointed at my arms.

His eyes doubled in size as he followed her finger to my birthmarks. He shot a scowl toward Kohath. "What is the meaning of this?" he demanded.

Kohath furrowed his eyebrows. "Do you mean her birthmarks?" Athaliah joined Kohath's side as she provided clarity. "The ancestors are to blame, and there is now a threat of war among witches." She bobbed her head toward me. "She is the result of their interference."

"Don't speak about me like I'm not here," I snapped. "I had no choice in any of this. If the two of you know anything about these marks, then say so!"

"Raven," Brandon gasped.

"It's fine, Brandon." The female vampire smiled at him before turning to me and taking my hands in hers. "Those are symbols of my bloodline, but it isn't possible. Yet here you stand, bearing my mark."

My mouth fell open, and I stumbled backward. "Who are you?" I asked.

She placed her hand on her chest and said, "I am Isis, goddess of rebirth and mistress of magic. Once upon a time, the universe worshipped me. It is true that I am still that goddess, but I am also a vampire god, responsible for the creation of vampirism. My efforts saved my husband." She smiled affectionately at him. "Osiris is the first vampire to walk the earth. He transformed nine of us with his blood, granting us, the Ten, immorality."

Words whirred inside my head: magic, vampires, nonhumans, witches, hosts, gods. I covered my mouth with my palm, suppressing a gasp. As I shook my head in denial, I thought, *how am I part of all of this?* I came looking for answers about my parents, not bizarre, inconceivable, unexplainable things. Would I have been better off not knowing where I came from and accepting my life as it was? But I owed the dead girls, witches like me, one last tribute. I had to right the wrong and show the world that a witch can be powerful and can make a difference. I had to be the one to take a stand and fight for what was right. I had to be brave.

With my head held high, I addressed Isis and Osiris. "There is more to the story than birthmarks." I glanced at Athaliah. "Athaliah is correct, the ancestors brought about this mess with their need to create a child. The person who offered to be their surrogate or host had a personal agenda: killing me and stealing my powers."

Eve gestured to Edith to push the wheelchair forward and inserted herself into the conversation. "It's true. After the host attempted to kill her baby, Raven, the ancestors imprisoned her and gloated that Raven's power could only be gained by unlocking a hidden code in her birthmarks. The host sacrificed herself to dark magic to escape the prison. Then the murders began— witches robbed of their blood and power. I, too, am a victim of her madness."

"I rescued Eve from the clutches of that deranged witch," Caleb explained. "Let's just say the witch wasn't thrilled with my interference."

"Caleb has a point. I know too much," Eve replied. "As she drained me, our blood mixed and I became privy to her thoughts. Therefore, I know firsthand that her intent is to consume power, and she will destroy Raven to do so."

"I saw the twisted side of that witch or host or whatever you choose to call her," Nico butted in with his two cents. "When she bit into her own baby, I knew I wasn't dealing with a normal mother. Like I said, I healed the baby and hightailed it out of that church with the baby. The only thing I could think of was to drop her off in front of a hospital. I waited until the doctors picked her up and then I left."

Isis's and Osiris's gazes shifted from person to person; yet their expressions were indistinguishable. There was no furrowing of the eyebrows, no widening of the eyes, no pursed lips, just expressionless, cool demeanors. The silence was so heavy, it hung like a fog in the room. It was as if they were two statues, immovable and unreadable, unlike everyone else in the room who felt the tension and dread of the unknown.

"I'm afraid this is all my fault. I encouraged Raven to seek out information from Eve and from Margarete. I'm the one who got everybody involved..." Brandon said, his voice fading to a whisper.

"It's not your fault. You were trying to help, and that means the world to me. I had no one before you." I squeezed his hand and kissed his cheek, forcing him to look at me. "Now I have this entire group helping me."

A slight smile crossed his lips as his eyes brightened. "Thank you, Raven."

Caleb huffed and waved a hand in the air. "It's not the time to be sentimental. We have an insane witch hunting us down. There are more important things to deal with than mushy feelings."

"Let them have their moment," Margarete said softly.

He rolled his eyes. "Not you too."

"Killjoy," she said, kissing him and then shooing him away.

I approached Isis. Her regal persona spread a tickle of intimidation down my arms, and my body shrank in upon itself. I attempted to sound confident, but my voice cracked as I said her name. Instantly I cleared my throat and tried again. "Isis."

"Yes, Raven," she replied.

My heartbeat pulverized my eardrums, but I ignored the chatter as I held my arms out and asked, "Do you see anything within my birthmarks that resembles a code? I only ask since these are symbols of your bloodline, I thought you might see something I don't."

Her gaze traveled up and down my arms several times before she shook her head. "No, I don't, not even with my vampire eyes." She turned to Eve, "Who said there was a hidden code?"

"The witch behind the murders. It was what the ancestors told her. I was able to read her mind when our blood mixed."

"I say we demand the appearance of these pesty ancestors and force the code out of them," Caleb concluded with a curt nod.

"That solution presents a problem as they are no longer living," Osiris pointed out. "Even as the Ruler of the Dead, I cannot force them to appear."

Caleb nudged Margarete forward. "The spirit world is Margarete's area of expertise. She may be able to help."

Margarete flashed a look of daggers toward Caleb. "I have a connection to the spirit world but I am not powerful enough to evoke the appearance of the ancestor witches."

"I'm a medium, Wiccan, and psychic," Eve revealed, "and even I cannot compel the ancestors to come forward."

"And you're too weak and need your rest," Edith scolded before Eve waved her away.

Isis raised her perfect brows as she tapped her foot. "Have you all forgotten who I am? I am the Mistress of Magic, their founding mother. I am very capable of summoning them through my magic."

Osiris bowed to Isis, saying, "Forgive me, my dear wife. A summons from you will surely bring them to our aid."

Nico raised his hand to draw attention to himself. "Hey, ya know, I love a good witch spell, but this really has nothing to do with me so can I book?"

Kohath gestured toward the door. "Of course. You're free to leave."

Nico bowed his head and clasped his hands. "Thank you." Before they changed their minds, he bolted from the room.

"It's not fair for me to have all the fun. Margarete and Eve, please come join me," Isis said, waving them over.

Margarete's smile spread across her face as she joined hands with Isis. "Absolutely." she replied.

The sweet expression on Caleb's face conveyed a deep connection and unwavering support between them. His eyes sparkled with admiration and tenderness, showing he cared deeply about Margarete. I found this much more appealing than the sarcastic Caleb.

As Edith placed Eve's wheelchair beside Isis, Eve took hold of Isis's hand and said, "I wouldn't miss this for the world."

Margarete and Eve followed Isis's lead and closed their eyes.

Isis's voice rose with urgency, replacing her calm demeanor as she recited, "Ancestors of old, hear my voice. I invoke thee. From ashes to ashes, from bone to bone. I summon thee. From spirit to spirit, from flesh to flesh." She lifted her arms to the heavens, bringing Margarete's and Eve's with hers. "I evoke thee. My ancestors, I summon you back to me."

Isis, Margarete, and Eve chanted in unison. "Ancestors of old, hear my voice. I invoke thee. From ashes to ashes, from bone to bone. I summon thee. From spirit to spirit, from flesh to flesh. I evoke thee. My ancestors, I summon you back to me."

A gentle breeze blew through the room and swept my hair into my eyes. I swiftly brushed it out of the way, eager to see the ancient witches in their full glory. As the temperature plummeted, I shuddered and Brandon drew me close to his side. I savored the warmth of his body as I rubbed away the chill.

Shadows engulfed the Council's table, as if an artist dabbed in the air, filling in shapes and colors with their brush. Three women and four men appeared from the shadows, all carbon copies of each other. Long flowing hair, dark eyes, and clothed in dark cloaks. Their opaque forms obscured their true spirit, but I could see through them. As one of the men stepped forward, his movements flickered like a hologram. Were my eyes playing tricks on me? I rubbed them, blinked, and looked again.

"Did you see that?" Brandon whispered in my ear. "It's almost as if they can teleport or move at a speed our eyes can't track."

"I noticed that too," I whispered back.

The witches possessed a powerful aura and radiance that captured my attention. They were unlike anything I had seen before.

The man bowed his head in respect to Isis before speaking. "You requested our presence." His gaze settled on my arms before returning to Isis. "I see you have located her."

As Isis cocked her head, a wrinkle crept into her flawless brow. "What do you mean, located her?" she asked.

"Mistress, do you not recall our visions of Osiris's murder, the transition of the gods, the bloodbath of vampirism, and the end of witches?"

Osiris stepped between Isis and the male ancestor and argued, "These warnings were given long ago—a different era. At your request, we freely offered our blood, flesh, and bone to reverse our hunger." Osiris paused and gestured toward the Council. "We gave birth to the Old Ones, as you advised. They govern our bloodlust, and the witches had no misfortune." He scanned the room again as he asked, "What do warnings from the past have to do with the present?"

"The reason is standing in this room," he explained with a rigid finger pointing at me. "Her creation was imminent to bring balance to the supernatural realm."

"Well, that's a tough sell since the host you selected started a war," Caleb quipped with his usual sarcasm.

"It was her pledge that clouded our judgment," he said, holding his head high.

"Not to mention, Raven can't use her power because of the code you imposed on her."

In a furrow of his brow, he cocked his head and asked, "What code?"

Eve accused, "The one you hid inside her birthmarks."

"No such code was hidden."

The focus in the room shifted to Eve.

"I was in her head and read her thoughts," Eve insisted, defending herself. "She believes Raven's birthmarks contain a hidden code because of what you all said to her."

In a display of defiance, the male witch shook his head. "We have no explanation for such a statement. It seems like a baseless assumption."

Until now, I had no say in the decisions that shaped my life. They made choices that left me feeling powerless and longing for control. For the first time, I was determined to take charge of my life. After pushing my way through Eve, Caleb, Isis, and Osiris, I stood before the flickering ancestors to make my case. "I beg to differ. The battle to master my magic is a daily struggle. I hit a brick wall if I try anything complicated. If what you say is true, and I'm supposed to prevent some war, why am I denied access to my own magic?"

A hushed tone filled the room as the ancestors turned their backs on us and whispered to each other. I studied their bewildered expressions. Had Eve misunderstood the host? As I glanced at Eve, her forehead was covered in sweat and her eyelids hung heavy. She groaned and doubled over in her wheelchair. She was struggling to remain conscious, and I knew she was in pain. My heart sank, and I felt helpless as I watched her suffer.

"That's enough! I have to take her back to her room," Edith snapped and hurriedly wheeled Eve out of the room. As the door closed, Eve's protest faded and silence followed. The ancestors continued their private huddle unscathed.

Athaliah strode up to the ancestors and clapped her hands loudly. "Time is of the essence. Do you have an answer or not?"

Athaliah's abrupt approach forced them apart, and this prompted the male witch to speak. "We believe we know what has hindered Raven's magical abilities. I can investigate and confirm, but we need Raven's consent to proceed."

Although I crossed my arms tightly to form a barrier between me and the ghost-like ancestor, I nodded in agreement.

"May I place my fingertips against your temples?" he asked, as his body flickered in front of me.

The question of whether I could trust him swirled through my mind. I looked at Isis. She was their leader. She knew them better than anyone. "Should I let him?" I asked.

"He won't harm you, and you deserve to know the answer," she replied firmly.

My eyes landed on the witch. "Yes, you may."

Several bright pulses of light emanated from his fingers, caus-ing a tingling sensation to spread across my forehead and scalp. Under the witch's spell, I relaxed my guard and allowed him full access to my mind. A sudden surge of power jerked my head for-ward, and my vision shifted to a strange world made of swirl-ing colors and shapes. I could feel my consciousness expanding beyond my physical body, as if I had tapped into some kind of cosmic energy.

As the glow dimmed, the witch released me and revealed, "Your magic will become independent only after your parents grant you permission."

"My parents?"

"Yes," He affirmed, nodding toward Isis and Osiris.

My gaze grew wide as I gawked at him. "What?" I asked, staggering backwards.

A look of shock filled Brandon's eyes as he grabbed onto me, steadying me.

Margarete, the Council, and even Caleb stared blankly at the ancestors in an eerie silence.

Osiris shattered the silence, shouting, "You created a child with our DNA?"

"We were at liberty to make use of your offerings as we saw fit. Nineteen years ago, we made a decision, and we have witnessed the consequences of that decision. Regardless, any magical beings who fail to abide by our decision will face our wrath. We must be vigilant and never forget our duty and responsibility to protect our coven and our people. Once we were witches and will be again because of her." He gestured toward me. "She was created to reign over mystical power and end the war against witches."

Osiris's lips flared with rage as he accused, "A war you started by planting our seed in a psychopath witch!"

The thought that I was the daughter of Isis and Osiris suddenly sent nausea coursing through my body. It wasn't physically impossible. It was impossible unless...I shook the thought away. I am still human. This can't be true. I am not some ancient being with mystical powers. I am just a regular person, and I can't possibly be part of an ancient prophecy. I can only hope that they're wrong and that this is all just a dream.

Again, a burst of air blew my hair into my face. While tucking it behind my ears, I caught sight of Isis barreling straight for the ancestor. Her nostrils flared and her lips curled as she bared her deadly fangs. Her hand encircled his ghostly neck as she lifted him off the ground. "You don't have the right to play God!" She raised him above her head, and he gasped as he struggled to escape.

I froze with fear and held my breath. I couldn't tell if she was disgusted with me or him. I searched for a way to intervene, but my body refused to react. If someone more powerful than me did not intervene, her rage would kill him.

Osiris must have heard my thoughts and shoved her hands away from the man. As he fell to the ground clutching his neck, the other ancestors gathered around him. As if the ancestors melted into the walls, they vanished, leaving no trace behind.

Osiris pointed at me. "Isis, look at our daughter's expression. She's terrified."

Her gaze shifted to me, and her expression softened. "I'm sorry, Raven. I'm no—"

A dark shadow covered the room as the temperature plummeted. Uncontrollable shivers gripped me. I pulled on my jacket and rubbed my arms, trying to keep warm. My breath hovered in front of me, and my teeth chattered so loudly I could not speak. We all needed to get out of the room before something horrible happened. I was too terrified to move. My mind and body refused to listen to my pleas to escape, no matter how hard I tried.

"What's going on here?" asked one Council member as he peered around the room.

A blinding white light erupted in the middle of the room, forcing everyone to shield their eyes. Sparks flew through the air, leaving scorch marks and a faint burning smell as they ricocheted off the walls. A shadowy figure appeared in the fading light, its surrounding air crackling with a dark aura that made the hairs on my neck stand on end. Caleb grabbed me in his arms and flew upward. His grip was firm and strong, holding me securely as we hovered effortlessly in the air. The floor seemed far below, a distant speck in the vast expanse of the room.

The figure stood in the center, shifting into a woman with long reddish-brown hair. A snarl rippled across the woman's lips as her face contorted with rage. Her black robe billowed around her, giving off an eerie presence. Her crazed blue eyes glared at Caleb and me, and the room grew colder.

My pulse thumped with panic as I realized the witch had found me. The piercing look in her eyes made my skin crawl. Caleb had saved me from becoming her next victim, and I shuddered in relief. He scowled at the witch, warning her, and acted as a shield between us.

"You're a fool if you think I can't fly," she shouted at us.

Caleb's grip tightened, and we soared higher. The woman's laughter echoed through the room as we ascended.

"Listen, witch, you're a fool if you think you can match my speed." He spun to the right, searching the floor, yelling, "Kohath, it's her. Take her."

Margarete tucked Brandon behind her, guarding him, as Kohath, Osiris, Isis, and Athaliah surrounded the witch.

"Let's talk this through," Kohath said with a calm, soothing voice, "No one needs to be hurt."

Her gaze remained fixed on Caleb and me. "I have come for what is mine." She pointed at me. "Bring her to me."

"Not a chance, freak."

"If you take what's mine, I'll take what's yours." The witch grinned and stepped back, her eyes flashing with power. A brilliant glow framed her body as she waved her arms in a large circle, mumbling an unidentifiable language. She snapped her fingers, sending smoke billowing into the room. The vapours had an odd blue tint, and ancient symbols swirled through the fumes. Instantly, darkness enveloped the room, leaving behind unbearable silence.

The only evidence of the witch's powerful spell was fumes rising from the burned floor. Caleb and I, the only survivors, were haunted by the unanswered question of where she took everyone.

Chapter 7

Caleb stood in front of the Council's empty table, his gaze blazing downward, his hands planted firmly on its surface. His voice reverberated through the chamber as he clenched his jaw. "I will not be intimidated by that grudge-bearing witch!" After a moment of pause, he declared unmercifully, "I will tear her apart limb by limb if she harms even a hair on Margarete's head. I will not hesitate to avenge her. This witch has no idea what kind of wrath I am capable of. I will make sure that she pays for her actions." He gritted his teeth and screamed in frustration as his fists struck the marble, cracking it and sending splinters flying across the surface.

I hung onto my shaking body as I swallowed the lump in my throat. Despite my brain's warning to run away from him, my feet ignored it. I stood frozen, my gaze fixed on him, praying he wouldn't devour me. He stepped closer, his eyes piercing through me, making my heart race. I trembled uncontrollably, and my mind went blank. Paralyzed by fear, I choked out, "Please don't hurt me."

"Raven, I saved your life. I won't harm you. We have to work together and get Margarete back."

I took a deep breath and squared my shoulders. "You mean, get everyone back? She has Brandon. He's human. How can he protect himself from such evil? What if she hurts him or the others?"

His eyes focused on mine as he said, "I won't let that happen. Brandon is smart and knows how to take care of himself, and we're going to get everyone back, unscathed. Any chance you know where this witch disappeared to?"

As I uttered the word "No," I cringed at my own weakness.

"Let's talk to Eve. Her connection with the witch may still be viable, and hopefully she'll have a location."

My world crumbled around me. Watching everyone disappear was a devastating experience that forced me to confront my weaknesses. I knew I had to stay strong and find the courage to fight the witch and restore balance to my world. It was my responsibility to get everyone back and to stop the witch's plan.

"Where did Edith take Eve?" I asked.

"The third floor is the only option. Hang on, though, while I reach out in thought." Momentarily, he closed his eyes. "I'm right. Let's go."

He gracefully leapt across the polished wooden floor with agile movements and defied gravity. He propelled me forward, his hand firmly wrapped around mine, his grip firm yet gentle. The stairs didn't interest him. We flew up to the third floor and down the dimly lit hallway. As we traveled the hallway, the walls blurred before we reached a door. After knocking twice and not waiting for an answer, he entered. We walked into a room sparsely furnished with a hospital-like bed in one corner and a chair next to it.

Eve lay motionless in the hospital-like bed and was hooked up to an IV, dripping ruby-red blood into a vein in her pasty white arm. A monitor at her bedside broadcast a steady beep. Edith adjusted the IV bag, ensuring steady flow. She glanced up and immediately shooed us away. "She needs to rest. Whatever it is can wait."

"'Fraid not. That damn witch showed up and took off with the entire Council, the gods, Margarete, and Brandon."

Edith's eyes widened in shock. "What?! How is that possible?"

Caleb moved her aside to get to Eve, then he shook his head. "I don't know, and that's why we need Eve's help. He leaned over Eve and raised his voice. "Eve, can you hear me? Wake up."

Eve's eyelids fluttered open as she stared blankly at her surroundings. As she regained her senses, she focused on Caleb and me. Her expression of dread deepened as she realized something had happened to the others. "Is something wrong? What's happened?"

"I'd say. That witch showed up, and it's devastating," Caleb explained with genuine concern. "As you said, she's after power and Raven. I protected Raven, but everyone else in the room suffered. The witch cast an abduction spell, grabbing everyone and disappearing. I think we underestimated her."

Eve's eyes doubled in size as she sat upright, trying to make sense of the situation. "You mean they vanished, everyone? Even Isis and Osiris?"

Caleb nodded solemnly. "Yes, all in one sweeping motion."

"To capture the gods, she must have immense power and strength, much more than I thought. We must act quickly before she succeeds in any wrongdoing. The consequences could be catastrophic."

An overwhelming amount of emotions flooded my brain, triggering mental numbness that trickled down into my legs. I stood in the corner, my mind and body shutting down, though I wanted to run and escape, my muscles refused to move. I felt paralyzed, unable to do anything except stand there and take it all in. I was trapped in an endless loop of panic and fear.

"Oh, there's more," Caleb said with an exaggerated nod. "As soon as you left the chamber, the ancestors dropped a bombshell: Raven is the child of Isis and Osiris, and she must have their approval before she can unleash the full potential of her magic. It is imperative that we devise a revised plan to counteract the witch without Raven's magic. Otherwise, we could suffer further losses."

Eve's eyes widened and her mouth formed an "O" shape as she gasped for words. After several seconds, she blurted, "Raven's parents are Isis and Osiris? Unless the laws of nature have changed, that's impossible."

"Impossible or not, they're her parents, but more importantly, we have to find them. Do you know the witch's location?"

"I really wish everyone would stop talking about me as if I were invisible." I interrupted. "My parents are Egyptian gods turned vampire gods. I don't even know if I'm human or not. Plus, I'm the one being hunted by that psycho witch who just swooped up everyone to get to me. So, cut me some slack."

Caleb nodded. "Point taken, but the fact that I can smell you proves you are human, or part human."

"Thank God!" I exclaimed as I splayed my hand over my heart.

"I see your human aura as well," Eve observed, "but now a remarkable glow surrounds you, suggesting that you are a hybrid."

The concept of a hybrid was a total mystery to me. How could I be both human and immortal if my parents were gods? Did it have something to do with the host being human? I dismissed that thought immediately. I was not born from her. She was merely a host. So where did the human part come into play?

Caleb's voice interrupted my thoughts. "Having settled that, can we move on to finding the witch? I intend to get Margarete back." I started to interject but he held up his hand. "And everyone else." He looked at Eve. "Where do you think she would have taken them?"

As her eyes shifted upward, Eve said, "I'm trying to recall the images I saw when our blood mixed. I don't remember seeing a house or building of some sort. I do remember trees and water."

"That could be anywhere."

"I'm sorry. That's all I remember."

Caleb's posture sagged before he recovered and stood tall. "That's all right. We'll find another way." He turned toward the door.

"Wait," Eve called out. "I remember a cave surrounded by trees."

"I'll work with that. Raven, let's go."

Eve threw the blanket aside and struggled to the edge of the bed. "I'm coming too."

"You are most certainly not," Edith objected.

Caleb reacted with no qualms as he said, "No offense, Eve, but in your condition, you'd only slow us down, and I'm not putting your life at risk that way."

With the speed of light, he grabbed my arm and dragged me out of her room without waiting for a response from her. We were back inside the Council's chamber before I could blink. He sat me in a chair, then paced the room, mumbling to himself. I wasn't sure whether to share my thoughts or remain silent. I chose silence.

A fourth loop around the room brought him to a grinding halt as his eyes widened. "It's time for reinforcements."

"More vampires?"

"Not quite." He studied me with narrowed eyes. "You've definitely been on a supernatural adventure, but things are about to get real."

I laughed out loud. "Oh, so all that chaos was pretend?"

"Ha! The kid's version is over. Only adults can advance to the next level. Are you ready to play?"

"Just tell me."

"I messaged Jaffa, a fire demon."

Without the chair holding me upright, my legs would have collapsed. "What?"

"She's trustworthy. You'll be fine. Though, she does travel quickly so not a lot of time to become acclimated to the idea." He waved me forward. "We'll meet her in the foyer."

"Do I have a choice?"

"If I didn't trust her, I wouldn't have asked for her help. Come on."

He whisked me away again. I was lost in a blur until he set me down in the center of a circular foyer. Three antique teardrop chandeliers illuminated an ornate gold ceiling as European marble tiles adorned the sparse and spacious room. As I took in the beautiful and unique space, I gazed in awe at the vibrant green vines dangling from the ceiling like living waterfalls. Turning around, I saw a pair of ice blue eyes peering back at me. White dreadlocks tumbled over her armored shoulders. As the chandelier's light reflected off the armor, a shimmering glow spread across her charred face. Her footsteps echoed through the empty foyer, emphasizing her authority and presence.

Fear and amazement washed over me as my eyes locked on this creature standing in front of me. Her piercing gaze burned through my soul, and I couldn't help but step back, overwhelmed by her presence.

"Who's the newbie?"

I meekly raised my hand, my voice trembling as I replied, "I'm the newbie, Raven."

She introduced herself with a slight smirk, "I am Jaffa."

"I appreciate you coming so quickly, Jaffa," Caleb said, shooing me out of the way. "We have a situation that calls for a locator spell."

"Again? You vampires seem to have a habit of losing each other. Who is it this time?"

"Well, Isis and Osiris are the repeat offenders. However, there are others. Brandon, Kohath, the entire Council, along with Mar… Margarete," he struggled with her name while gripping his chest. A wince escaped his lips as he caught his breath.

Her ice blue eyes sharpened. "How did this happen?"

In a fit of rage, he cursed, "This damn witch abducted them." His voice failed him, and he clenched his jaw.

Stepping forward, I continued for him. "It's about me. In summary, the ancestors created me from Isis's and Osiris's DNA, but they needed a surrogate to carry their creation to full-term. I was born with powers I still do not understand. Nineteen years ago that witch gave birth to me, then tried to kill me. The ancestors imprisoned her for her betrayal. Recently she escaped and has been killing witches to absorb their power, searching for me. My search for my parents led me here, where she tracked me. She demanded my surrender, but Caleb and the others protected me. I'm responsible for her retaliation and apprehending everyone. Supposedly, I am the only one who can stop her so I must find a way to defeat her and protect the world from her evil plans."

Her eyes flicked between me and Caleb with a hint of amusement. "It never ceases to amaze me the situations you people get into, but I will find them and bring them home."

"I'm coming with you," Caleb insisted.

"I appreciate your offer, but I will handle this on my own," she replied firmly.

With a stubborn stance, Caleb folded his arms. "I can't just sit around and wait. Besides, I'm not asking for your permission. I'm telling you I'm coming."

"It's your job to keep Raven safe."

As he slumped into a chair, clutching his head, his whole body sighed.

"What about the rest of the Ten?" she asked, resting her hand on his shoulder. "Are they aware? Maybe you should have them join you here."

His head shook in disapproval. "They'll fly off the handle. Declare war. Put everyone at risk. Hence, the reason I called you. You're levelheaded, cool, calm, and collected. You're not affected by emotions. The Ten will get them killed. You will save them."

With determination in her voice, she said, "I'm going to find them. You stay here and watch out for anything suspicious."

He stared intensely at me before taking a deep breath and steeling himself for the task ahead. "I will keep her safe," he affirmed. "Jaffa, you know what needs to be done. Don't let me down."

Caleb and I were left alone as she strode away, back straight and head held high. Her strength sent a wave of relief through me. For the first time in days, I felt a sense of hope. I got the feeling she would do whatever it took to accomplish her mission.

Chapter 8

Two days had passed since Jaffa left. Throughout the Haven, a hover of tension and uncertainty lingered in the air. The Council's staff took excellent care of us, despite their trepidation over their missing leaders. Caleb was beside himself, pacing back and forth like a caged lion, and his unease only heightened mine. While he cared about immortals, I worried about Brandon. Being a human, how would he fare against a powerful witch? I couldn't shake the feeling that something bad would happen, and I could do nothing more but wait and hope that everyone made it out safely.

When I was alone in my room, I switched on my cell phone. A flood of messages from my adoptive parents blew up my phone. In response, I told them the truth, texting back that I was searching for my biological parents. As soon as I hit send, I turned off my cell phone and stepped away, trembling. I knew those words would be difficult for them, but for me, the weight of guilt floated away, and relief took its place. I could breathe again now that I'd come clean.

Caleb barged into my room, wide-eyed and frantic. "Don't do that. Don't disappear on me like that," he snapped.

"Do you knock? This isn't the first time I've come here for privacy."

"Raven, privacy is non-existent right now. I turned around, and you were gone. We don't know what that witch is planning. Until Jaffa returns, we must remain vigilant and stay together."

Our conversation was interrupted by a knock at the door. We paused, uncertain as to who was on the other side. Uncertainty pounded in my chest as I awaited what news lay beyond the door. Despite my nerves, I had to point out, "At least someone knocks."

As he turned the doorknob, he smirked, saying, "Don't be such a smartass."

I felt my stomach churning with suspense as Teresa stood in the doorway, her pale hands clasped tightly together. She took a deep breath and stared at him. An eerie silence filled the room. Caleb gazed at her with concern evident in his eyes. It was clear he understood the severity of the situation. He motioned for me to follow him as he entered the hallway.

"We have visitors," she said.

"Who's here?"

"Nephthys, Horus, Hathor, Hypatia, and Rick."

Caleb scraped his hand through his hair as he asked, "Is there any news of Jaffa?"

She shook her head.

With a look of disbelief and anger on his face, he sarcastically responded, "Wonderful. We'll have to appease the high and mighty."

"Who are they?" I asked.

"You're about to find out." He faced Teresa. "Where are they?"

"In the foyer."

"Come on. I'll explain on the way, but I'm not in a hurry. We'll take a slow human approach."

A carpeted hallway lined with antique brass sconces led us to the mahogany staircase, with its intricate carvings and marble banister, leading to the foyer. The chandeliers in the foyer cast a rainbow of colors on those standing beneath them.

Caleb stopped, turned to me, and explained, "Nephthys is the sister of Isis, Horus is the son of Isis and Osiris, Hathor is Kohath's maker, Hypatia is Kohath's sister, and Rick used to be Brandon's friend before he turned. Plus, Nephthys, Horus, and Hathor are members of the Ten. Expect drama."

A strange combination of fear and fascination quickened my pulse. I had a family, not just a mother and father, but also a brother and an aunt. I also had a whole other world I had no idea existed. Through them, I would gain a deeper understanding of who I am and where I came from, no matter how challenging it may be. Finding my voice, I uttered, "I have a brother and an aunt?"

"Yes, but keep your excitement in check. They're gods after all."

"I have no idea what that means."

"It means they're unpredictable and dangerous. We're about to break the news that a psycho witch has taken their loved ones and you're the daughter of Isis and Osiris. Both scenarios will be equally difficult for them to hear."

Neither my news nor the abduction news would be comforting. We all had a stake in annihilating the witch's plans. Caleb also had to explain why he kept them in the dark. Having been at the center of it all, I was not blameless either, so I had to accept responsibility for my actions. We needed to work together. "Maybe they can help locate the others," I said, trying to sound optimistic.

"Ha! Doubtful."

"They seemed pretty upset," Teresa advised.

Caleb rolled his head backward and sighed. "Where's a fire demon when you need one?" He shook out his hands and regained composure. "Let's get this over with."

He led the way down the stairs, followed by me and Teresa. As I glanced over at the vampires in the foyer, a female with jet-black hair covered in jewelry caught my attention. In many ways, she resembled Isis, and she possessed the same air of authority and power. I assumed Hypatia and Hathor were the other two females, one with long blonde curls and the other with unique chocolate brown hair. There was an imposing and intimidating energy between them, something only they could comprehend. It was clear that I was in the presence of beings far more powerful than I could ever understand. The two males: Horus or Rick, one with sandy colored hair hanging in his eyes, while the other had long and thick black hair. I was in awe of the strength and power they displayed.

As soon as they noticed us, the vampires flocked to Caleb. Even though they remained silent, their eyes blazed with fury. I had no idea who would win that battle. The stakes were very high for everyone. Caleb stood tall and unafraid as he faced them. It seemed like he had control over the situation, as if he knew something I didn't.

The Isis lookalike narrowed her gray-colored eyes at Caleb and demanded, "What happened to my sister?"

She's my aunt!

Without waiting for Caleb to respond, the sandy-haired male darkened his navy-colored eyes and declared, "I know you were the last to see my mother and father. Tell me where they are!"

And he's my brother!

"Can I respond?" Caleb asked, raising his hands.

The two stood silently, nodding and waiting for his response. Caleb looked back and forth between them for a few moments before finally speaking. "I purposely withheld their disappearance from you as I knew you would lack rationale. The fact is, I don't know where they are." His voice was measured and deliberate as he spoke. He paused, allowing the gravity of his words to sink in before continuing. "That's why I contacted Jaffa. She is capable of tracking down any target, no matter how well hidden they are, and she will find them without endangering their lives."

"And what about Kohath?" asked the blonde female as if she hadn't heard a word Caleb said. "We must unravel the mystery of his disappearance as well."

"Brandon is the only human among these missing immortals," the black-haired male said. "He is the most vulnerable."

The female with chocolate brown hair rested her hand on his back and assured, "We will find him—all of them."

The vampire was right, Brandon was most at risk, but should I share my feelings? Not that it would matter to them. I was just a mere human, disposable, insignificant, and a food source, but I had to be strong, no matter what. With a deep breath, I decided to speak up. "I'm worried about Brandon too."

I became their focal point, especially the black-haired male. His gaze narrowed as he studied me with a flurry of wrinkles running across his forehead. He relaxed slightly after the female next to him touched his forearm in a reassuring gesture. My future could be shattered by one wrong move. The mounting tension in the room accelerated my heartbeat, like a vampire's homing device. Would they attack me? Rather than standing there and doing nothing, I shielded myself from them by moving behind Caleb.

He squared his shoulders and met their gaze. "I apologize. I should have introduced everyone."

Taking a step to the side, Caleb gestured toward me as if he were displaying a trophy. Their intense gazes made me feel exposed and vulnerable, as though I were an insect under a microscope. As I stood before them, my palms began to sweat and I wondered if I truly was safe.

"Raven," Caleb pointed at the blonde, "this is Hathor, Kohath's maker." His hand moved to the female with jet-black haired. "This is Nephthys, Isis's sister." Caleb nodded toward the sandy-haired vampire standing next to her. "This is Horus, Isis and Osiris's son." He then motioned to the female with chocolate brown hair. "This is Hypatia, Kohath's sister." The vampire with black hair was his last stop. "And finally, we have Rick, Brandon's friend." Caleb put his hand on my shoulder as he said, "Everyone, this is Raven, the daughter of Isis and Osiris."

A hush fell over the room. Everyone froze. The vampires exchanged skeptical glances, their fangs glinting in the light as they whispered among themselves in disbelief. With my mortal appearance, how could I be the daughter of powerful deities like Isis and Osiris? Their eyes centered on me, determining whether I was their progeny or an elaborate hoax.

When I glanced down at my naked arms, I realized my birthmarks represented Isis's ancient power, passed down from generation to generation. They should have noticed, but I had to show them, explain what Isis said, especially to Nephthys and Horus. "Isis told me these were symbols of her bloodline." As I held my arms out, Isis's ancient power was clearly visible. The marks covering the surface of my arms, ensured that no one could doubt the strength and significance of my connection to Isis's bloodline.

Nephthys's gaze shifted to me, and I felt instantly judged. There was an undeniable intensity in her stare, as if she were looking straight through to my core. The room seemed to hold its breath, waiting for Nephthys to break the silence and reveal her trust or doubt.

"That's impossible," she said, shaking her head.
Doubt it was.

"'Fraid not," Caleb replied, validating my legitimacy. "Compliments of the ancestors."

Horus's chin jutted out, the muscles in his jaw clenching. "What does that mean?"

"The DNA of your parents was used to create Raven by the ancestral witches, to be precise."

Horus's navy-blue eyes pierced the depths of my soul, sending a chill coursing through my veins as I backed away, unable to take my eyes off him. He growled, baring his fangs and leaping into the air. I screamed as he locked me in his grasp, his powerful, razor-sharp fangs plunging into my flesh. A burning sting swelled in my throat as my own blood rushed down my neck.

He shot off the ground and jerked me upward against my will. Vampires below shouted, "Horus, no! Stop! Let her go! Are you insane?" Horus ignored them and continued to fly upward. I was doomed to a fate I could not control. He soared above the others at speeds that whipped my hair into my face. As his icy fingers gripped my arm, the chill penetrated my bones. I squinted my eyes against the wind, trying to see what was going on. With the ground rushing away from us, I knew I had to do something. I wasn't going to let him take my life.

A rush of adrenaline surged through my body, giving me a new sense of strength. Striking him in the chest with my fists and kicking my legs as hard as I could, I tried to break his grip. My retaliation infuriated him. In one motion, he grasped a handful of my hair, jerked my head backward and sunk his fangs deeper, gorging on my blood. As a numbing sensation spread through my limbs, I grew cold.

Out of the corner of my eye, I caught sight of Caleb hovering beside us. He snarled and curled his lips, showing his fangs. In a threatening tone, he warned, "If you hurt her, you're signing your own death warrant."

The god spun us around, taunting Caleb as we drifted toward the ceiling's highest point. His laughter echoed through the room as his power kept us in midair.

Caleb's eyes burned with anger as he glared at Horus. He opened his mouth, then pressed his lips into a rigid line. His nostrils flared, and his breathing became ragged.

To hell with words, it was time for action. I cried, "Help me, Caleb!"

Caleb's gaze shifted to me and he ordered, "Stay still."

He didn't have to say anything else; I knew to obey.

A wave of intense heat rushed up and over my head, aiming at Horus, bursting into flames as it struck him. Horus screamed and flailed his arms, trying to dodge the inferno. As he struggled against the blaze, he threw me aside, sending me tumbling through the air. My stomach flew into my throat as I squeezed my eyes shut and braced for impact. Strong arms wrapped around me, arresting my fall and I looked up into Jaffa's ice blue eyes.

"Don't worry, baby witch, I've got you," she said as we slowly descended to the ground, where Caleb was already waiting.

He stabbed his finger, drew blood, and smeared it on my neck. As my skin pulled together, closing the wound, the painful sting faded. Horus lay on the ground, his arms blistered by the fire, and his breathing labored and heavy. After struggling for a few seconds to rise to his feet, he crumpled onto the floor, his body shaking uncontrollably. Nephthys rushed to his side. Stroking his hair, she scowled at Jaffa. "You didn't have to burn him."

"He'll recover," Jaffa said, waving her away.

In a rage, Nephthys lunged forward at Jaffa, clenching her fists. Nephthys's eyes were wild and dark as she gritted her teeth and raised her fist to strike. Jaffa stood her ground, not even a flinch disturbed her calm but determined expression. In my next breath, Jaffa ignited her fiery aura, causing the armor to glow with a mesmerizing intensity. As orange flames danced around her body, she unleashed her primal strength, transforming into a deadly torch. Exercising her fierce rage, she hurled an inferno at Nephthys, immobilizing and crippling her. "Don't challenge me, vampire god!" Jaffa warned. "The weapons I use are now a thousand times more powerful than before. You can't defeat me. I am not threatened by the Ten anymore. If I were you, I would stand down."

Neither Nephthys nor Jaffa moved, their stares locked. Jaffa's dominance was undeniable. Her flames crackled, leaping higher in victory until the vampire god finally backed down, defeated. The standoff ended as Nephthys bowed her head to Jaffa and returned to tend to Horus. Jaffa had won the battle. Her flames dwindled, and her focus shifted to Caleb. "I've found them in the city of Anguith," she said.

In a blur, Caleb rushed forward, grabbing her hands. "Tell me they're alive?"

"Though their bodies hang motionless in the jagged Cave of Ashes, their hearts beat steadily and strongly," Jaffa answered calmly.

Caleb staggered backward, and his legs buckled beneath him. He tried to speak, but only shallow breaths came out of his mouth. Jaffa whispered something in his ear. He nodded weakly and then straightened his posture. With a determined look in his eyes, he demanded, "We must rescue them."

A strained expression crossed Jaffa's face as she shook her head. After a few moments of contemplation, she finally said, "The Cave of Ashes can only be reached through the Dead Forest. Unknown dangers lurk there. It is a dark and treacherous journey that not many can make."

"How did you manage this treacherous journey?" Hathor asked in a snide tone.

"My travels do not disturb the earth. My thoughts transport me; therefore, I am invisible, even to the supernatural."

"While we fly at unearthly speeds, our movements do impact the earth," Rick pointed out.

"Rick is right," Hypatia agreed. "The flight will be noticeable, especially to a powerful witch."

As they spoke, my gaze bounced back and forth between them. We all underestimated that witch. She had robbed countless bodies of blood and power, making her invincible. I was determined not to give up, even though I feared we wouldn't win, especially after she defeated two gods and restrained the entire Council. I had to figure out how to unlock my power and use it to save everyone.

"We must rescue them," Caleb repeated, breaking my concentration. "I'm counting on all of you. Are you with me?"

With a bounce in her step, Eve stepped into the foyer and asked, "With you on what?" In the soft light of the room, her sickly pale complexion vanished, and her eyes twinkled. As Eve recognized Rick, her eyes widened with excitement. "Rick, it's so nice to see you," she exclaimed as she ran toward him, embracing him.

Rick's mouth dropped open in disbelief. He couldn't find the words to respond. As he returned her embrace, his expression softened into a warm smile. After a few moments, he said,

"Eve, wow. It is wonderful to see you again, even in such difficult circumstances."

Taking a look around the room, she frowned and asked, "Where is everyone? And who are they?"

As I gawked at Eve, my mind raced with worry. Had she forgotten everything Caleb had said, or was it the blood loss? Had she lost so much blood that her brain was permanently damaged?

Everyone exchanged glances, waiting for someone else to speak up. The weight of unspoken words loomed over the room until Caleb broke it. His voice rippled with frustration as he said, "Clearly, you didn't grasp what we discussed earlier. So, let me repeat what I said." He clenched his teeth and struggled to control his voice. "That witch...kidnapped the entire Council, Isis, Osiris, Margarete, and Brandon, and now...she's holding them captive."

Eve's jaw fell open. "No, I don't remember. What? How?"

"She just zoomed in, scooped them up, and left."

My heart ached to watch Caleb's face contort with pain and anger. I owed him for protecting me from the witch. In the aftermath, he stood his ground and kept his word to Jaffa. "Caleb protected me. I'm grateful to him, but also sorry. They're all gone because of me."

Putting her arm around my shoulders, Eve said, "This is the witch's fault, not yours." Eve's eyes widened as she grabbed my arm and pushed me behind her and away from Jaffa. Her body trembled and she stuttered, "Wh-who are you?"

Jaffa's eyes gleamed with superiority as she assessed Eve's trembling form. A smirk tugged at the corners of her mouth as she said, "I am Jaffa—a fire demon summoned by Caleb to locate his missing comrades."

With a shrug of his shoulders, Caleb confirmed. "It's true."

Her fear faded away as she gazed at Jaffa. Eve was powerful, and she should be filled with courage and resolve. After all, she was a medium, Wiccan, and psychic who faced many creatures in her lifetime. This demon was just another challenge. Eventually, she said, "I'm Eve, Rick and Brandon's friend. I'm a medium, Wiccan, and psychic."

Jaffa bowed her head. "Given the unique circumstances we face, your supernatural skills could provide an invaluable advantage."

"Of course, I'll help in any way I can."

Rick nudged forward the female vampire who had remained by his side and introduced her to Eve. "This is Hypatia, Kohath's sister and my companion."

Eve smiled as she gently grasped Hypatia's hand. Hypatia returned the gesture.

Caleb approached Rick and waved him away, and then continued introductions. "Eve, meet Nephthys, Isis's sister. Horus is Isis and Osiris's son, and Hathor is Kohath's maker. Everyone, this is Eve."

Eve had a unique ability to communicate with spirits and tap into the supernatural realm, which fascinated the vampires and made her an ideal ally to locate their friends and rescue them. Eve's powers aligned with the vampires' interests, which led the vampires to accept her as a key member of their group. It is Jaffa who she turned to. Her eyes were fiery with determination. "You said Caleb asked you to locate them. Did you find them?"

"Of course."

After hearing Jaffa say those words again, Caleb rocked back and forth and pressed his lips together. The priority of his life was to rescue Margarete. A knot formed in my stomach as I watched him in distress, knowing I had no power to do anything about it. The words I wanted to offer were dying on my tongue as my voice caught in my throat. I was aware that we had no time to waste, but the realization deepened my sense of helplessness.

"Where did you find them?" Eve asked.

"In the Cave of Ashes," Jaffa replied.

"The Cave of Ashes?" Eve's face paled. She swallowed hard and choked on her words. "To–to get there, you have to go through the Dead Forest. It's cursed." She shuddered and whispered, "People go in and don't come out."

"I did witness human remains littered across the forest floor," Jaffa admitted.

The hairs on my arms rose. I shivered and brushed off the chill. I'd never heard of the Dead Forest and adding the word "cursed" to its resume didn't help either. Rather than use this place to reach the cave, it sounded like a place to avoid. I felt hopeless, like we were caught in a web of doom. With no way out, our fate seemed sealed. My only hope was that we could survive whatever lay ahead.

"All the more reason we need to rescue them," Caleb emphasized with a curt tone, not letting go of his goal to save Margarete. "We cannot let obstacles get in the way of our mission. The thing we need to fear is the witch's plans for her prisoners."

As Eve shook her head, she seemed determined to prove a point. In a strong and steady voice, she challenged, "If we become victims of the forest, we cannot help anyone."

As Caleb grasped at his hair in frustration, I thought he was going to lose his mind. "We can't leave them there!" he shouted.

"Magical creatures lurk in the forest shadows," Eve continued. "To survive forest trials, one must use all their courage and strength. It is forbidden to step on dry leaves, as they make a distinctive noise that may attract creatures. Only by gaining the forest spirits' permission and respecting their domain can one safely navigate the treacherous path that leads to the Cave of Ashes." Eve looked at me. "Only one person can embark on this journey. It must be you, Raven."

The room spun around me, disorienting my senses. My heart rate accelerated, and dizziness overwhelmed me. Grabbing Eve's arm, I steadied myself. After several deep breaths, I regained control. "You can't be serious!"

Caleb huffed at Eve. "It's inconceivable to expect a witch without powers to survive this perilous forest, let alone a deranged and powerful witch." Caleb tapped a finger to Eve's temple. "That blood loss must have damaged some of your brain cells."

As Eve spoke, she seemed unaware of the insult Caleb hurled at her. "I'm serious, but not Raven as she is now, but Raven with all her strength."

An air of frustration reverberated from every direction. A silent stare filled Hypatia's eyes. Nephthys shook her head, sighing. Horus slowly rose to his feet, frowning in confusion. Hathor threw her hand in the air as if reasoning with a mortal was pointless. Jaffa grinned, and Rick addressed Eve, "Do you have a plan for Raven to gain her powers? According to her, her parents would have to give her permission."

Her brow furrowed as she tapped her fingertips on her lips in contemplation. "When did this happen? Something I missed again?"

Caleb responded before I could speak. "In fact, you did. As I explained before, the ancestors revealed that special fact after Edith whisked you away. Since Isis and Osiris are down for the count, hanging in some bat cave, they won't offer their approval anytime soon."

She shook her head slowly, as if trying to dislodge any lingering cobwebs in her mind, and then spoke. "What about her adoptive parents," Eve proposed. "Could they give approval?"

I stared at her in disbelief, trying to process her absurd question. I couldn't possibly agree to putting my adoptive parents' lives at risk. "I will not involve my adoptive parents in this!"

Horus abruptly regained his strength and pushed me aside. His forehead throbbed with a vein that threatened to burst as he hurled fury at Jaffa. "How dare you set a god on fire?"

With one hand on her hip, she fired back, "And you shouldn't have fed off your own sister."

He glared at Jaffa, balling up his fists and trembling with rage. A menacing growl escaped his lips as he charged forward. Nephthys, with herculean strength, gripped Horus by the arms and held him back. Her piercing eyes glowed with power and authority, boring into Horus's soul as she demanded the truth. "The truth lies in the blood you drank. Is she your sister and my niece?" Nephthys's calm demeanor conveyed the message she would not relent until the truth was revealed.

He spat out the word as if it were poison. "Yes."

"Then we must embrace her as family."

His dark and icy gaze drifted toward me. "I don't need a sister."

Her breath caught in her throat as she gasped, "Horus!"

Why he despised me, I didn't know. Maybe it was jealousy. He was an only child, and all their love was given to him. Now, he must share it with me. I threatened his perfect world. I could see it in his eyes. He would probably never accept me, but I wouldn't give up that easily. I wiped the sweat off my palms and said in a quiet voice, "Well, I'd love to have a big brother. Let me prove to you that I'm loyal and trustworthy."

"Hmph," he replied, yet my hope was renewed when I saw the darkness soften in his eyes.

My aunt embraced me tightly and kissed both cheeks. The smell of lavender and rosemary wafted through her hair. I felt relaxed in her arms, as if I had known her all my life. She released me saying, "Family means everything to us."

Jaffa cleared her throat, attracting attention. "I hate to break up this family reunion, but Raven's powers and the forest demand our attention. Isis and Osiris are incapacitated, and if her adoptive parents are out, we must find another way to access her magic. Moreover, who goes into the forest?"

The blonde goddess heaved an exaggerated sigh and said, "I'm over all of this, and I'm about to pursue them myself. Stop the bickering and just make a decision."

Hypatia shook her head and rolled her eyes. From the way she and Hathor looked at each other, I sensed tension between them. The rivalry was evident. There was something deeper going on. Kohath was the link between them. Could it be over him?

Horus mumbled something, and Jaffa caught it. "What about her blood? Speak up, god. Tell us what you know."

"Horus, what else have you learned from her blood?" Nephthys asked.

A sigh fell from his lips, and then he admitted, "Her adoptive parents cannot grant permission. They are not of her bloodline. It's her blood that will light the fuse to her magic. It must be awakened by its creator, my parents."

I heard Caleb whisper, "Margarete," as he hung his head and wrapped his arms around his torso.

"Don't give up." Jaffa waved a finger at Caleb. "We'll find a way to get everyone back." She glanced at me. "May I peek inside your mind?"

What did it mean to have a demon peering into my brain? Could I protect my innermost thoughts and feelings from such an intrusive force? A chill swept over me as I thought about the situation. I was completely vulnerable. Could I trust her? Did I have a choice?

"It's just a harmless peek, don't worry."

Caleb approached me and took my hands, squeezing them. His eyes were full of emotion, and his voice was filled with sadness. "As much as I know it's selfish of me, please let her."

"Um, yeah, I guess so."

The demon stood before me, and the vampire stood to my left. My heart pounded as I gazed into her ice-blue eyes. Power radiated from her fingers as she wove them into my hair and pressed them against my scalp. A wave of adrenaline and fear swept over me. Taking a deep breath, I took a leap of faith and put my trust in her.

Her eyes flashed with blinding light, and I threw my hand up to block it. A popping sound struck my ears, and stinging heat spread down my arms as my birthmarks turned orange-red. Sparks flew out of my birthmarks, and the smell of burning flesh clung to my nose. I winced and gritted my teeth, expecting the pain to subside, but it grew more intense with each passing second. Tears streamed down my face as I screamed in agony. I was soaked in sweat and it cascaded off my body, the droplets hitting the floor and hissing.

I collapsed to the ground as Jaffa released me, my skin still burning. Relief washed over me as the pain slowly dissipated.

Despite what she had done to me, I managed to survive. It filled my body with warmth, strength, and power I'd never known before. My arms caught my attention. Several birthmarks disappeared!

They stared at me, shocked. Although I couldn't tell if Jaffa's actions or my vanishing birthmarks promoted their behavior, I didn't care. I pointed at Jaffa and cried, "That wasn't a harmless peek!"

She kneeled beside me and placed her hand on my shoulder. "I apologize for the pain, but I found a backdoor. It was imperative that I acted quickly before it closed. After fighting your internal bloodline, I awakened half of your power before it shut me out. With this power, you can pass through the Dead Forest without falling victim to its devious tricks."

Seeing the energy radiating from me, I pushed myself upright and stood in awe as newfound strength surged through me. My surroundings blurred, and I became lighter, free from gravity's grip. My magical power carried me higher and higher into the air. Uncertainty filled me as I mastered levitation, but how? My pulse quickened as I realized I was vulnerable against the strange power I had been given. I closed my eyes, hoping it was all a dream, but when I opened them I was still floating. My task was to master these new abilities. The thought of not being able to control them terrified me.

A loud voice below sent me plummeting to the ground. As I spiraled downward, air rushed from my lungs. Strong arms once again stopped my rapid descent. It was Horus. As we glided to the ground, my head ached and my pulse accelerated. I continued to shake as he set me on my feet. Nephthys led me to one of the chairs while Eve handed me a glass of water. As I sipped the cold liquid, my racing heart slowed.

Jaffa applauded. "Well done. You've mastered levitation."

With a shrug, I replied, "No, I didn't. That just happened. I have no idea how I managed to do that."

Jaffa smiled. "You don't need to know how. You just need to trust in yourself and your power."

"Sorry, Smokey," Caleb retorted. "She'll need more than that advice to succeed."

"You'll go up in smoke if you call me Smokey again."

"I'm just trying to help her out. You don't have to be so defensive."

"I don't like being called Smokey. I'm not a bear."

Caleb was a sarcastic ass despite his devastation after Margarete's abduction. He had a point, though. Trusting in my abilities wasn't enough, especially when traveling through a creepy forest that was likely to hold me prisoner. I took a deep breath and reminded myself that I had a mission to complete and couldn't let fear take control. All my focus and courage had to be about surviving the forest. I was determined to bring them all back to safety. Raising my voice, I asked, "How do I get to this forest, and is there a path that I should follow once I'm there?"

Caleb rolled up his sleeves and rubbed his hands together. "I'm coming with you."

The mighty Horus replied with a curt nod. "I'm coming too."

Rick tossed his name into the hat. "And me."

Eve leapt forward, waving her arms crisscross-style. "Have you all lost your minds? If your goal is to kill everyone, then follow Raven. If you want them to live, then stay here."

As Jaffa stood tall and thrust her shoulders back, she agreed with Eve. "The more of you who insist on going, the more Raven and the task are put at risk."

My aunt stood still, her eyes unfocused and her lips parted. She seemed in her own world. After a few moments, her gaze sharpened and she smiled. She walked over to me, taking my hands in hers, and said softly, "It is your journey, and yours alone. You are capable of much more than you realize. Trust your abilities. You can do this."

After looking into her eyes, a surge of courage and strength rose within me. It was as if she understood what I needed. I took a deep breath and stood tall. I gathered my courage, determined to face whatever danger lay in the forest.

Chapter 9

As Jaffa traced her fingertips across my forehead, she etched the forest's location inside my brain. The visual map unfolded in my mind's eye, showcasing the twists and turns of the Dead Forest. Shadows danced among the trees, their branches swaying in anticipation, adding another layer of intrigue and danger to the already daunting Dead Forest.

My quest to reach the Dead Forest was enhanced when Eve joined in after Jaffa's mind-melding. Her voice rose and fell as she chanted a transportation spell. "Ancient spirits, I summon you. Lighten the darkness and echo through the night. Make the Dead Forest visible with all your might."

As the words left Eve's lips, a powerful sensation surged through my body, propelling me forward with incredible force. The spell transported me beyond the boundaries of our planet, into the vastness of space. The stars, once distant and insignificant, now gathered around me, their radiant glow enveloping me in a warm embrace. Every breath I took was filled with the cosmic energy of the universe, amplifying my connection to the very fabric of existence. My journey was guided by the stars, witnessed by the moon, and communicated by the wind until my feet touched the ground.

Contrary to the weightless space, the ground felt solid beneath me. The stars, still visible in the blue sky, twinkled with intensity, confirming the significance of my journey. I adjusted to the normal parameters of gravity, reminding myself of my physical form.

My euphoria was shattered as the Dead Forest appeared before me. Taking in my surroundings, the forest itself seemed suspended in time—as if I'd traveled through a wormhole to another dimension. The trunks of interlocking trees blocked the forest opening. Eerie whispers rushed forward from the depths of the forest, calling my name and beckoning me to enter. My heartbeat thumped against my ribs as I stumbled away from the darkness that lurked beyond the trees. Goose bumps pinched my flesh as I ran, my breath coming in short gasps, and I didn't dare to look back. I stopped only when I was sure I was safe.

The sun shone brightly against a pale blue sky as I rubbed off the chill from my arms. The rays cascaded down on the blanket of greenery around me, stretching out for miles. In contrast, gloomy shadows surrounded the opening of the forest as if the trees had absorbed all the light. Moss clung to the old bark, and a thick fog hovered just above the ground, obscuring what lay beyond. Even the grass halted at its edge, as if it did not want to enter. A stench of damp earth and decay drifted toward me. Despite my fear, I had to walk through the forest to reach the Cave of Ashes. Everyone was counting on me, and supposedly my magic would defeat the witch, but I wasn't so sure.

The foul odor intensified as I approached the entrance, making me gag. Covering my nose with my jacket, I forced myself to continue. My eyes watered as I drew closer. The smell was unlike anything I had ever experienced. It was impossible to compare it, but I couldn't help but think of dead bodies, though I had no idea what one would smell like. In that moment, I wished Caleb or Jaffa were by my side. I'd give anything to embody their power and courage. What if I didn't succeed? What if I was unable to save everyone from the witch? What if she killed me too? With a deep breath, I shook off my nerves and gathered my strength. I could do this. I *had* to do this.

At the forest's opening, I peered into the darkness. A damn flashlight would be helpful. Surely I could summon up something as simple as a flashlight. With my palms held high, I closed my eyes and envisioned light. "My ancient ancestors, I appeal to you," I chanted as the vision in my mind's eye grew brighter. "My call for guidance comes at this hour. Fill me with magic, both old and new. Let me make light out of darkness with my power."

A brilliant glow penetrated my eyelids. I opened my eyes to find a magical orb swirling in the palm of my hand, radiating beams of fiery light around me. Staring at the object, I stood absolutely still, then covered my mouth with my free hand and muffled a squeal. My small triumph was the strength I needed. As though I could conquer the world, I entered the forest with my head held high.

Dry leaves crackled under my shoes, and I recalled Eve's warning. "It is forbidden to step on dry leaves, as they make a distinctive noise that may attract creatures." At once, I zigzagged between them and the twisted tree roots covering the ground. Their massive trunks spiraled upward, towering toward the heavens while their branches bent down into an interlocking canopy overhead. The light from my magical orb illuminated skeletal remains scattered about the forest floor, partially covered by leaves and dirt.

The snapping of branches filled my ears. As I turned, I noticed a silhouette in the distance. I aimed my orb at it, and it remained motionless. Was it a person? The obscure form ducked out of sight only to reappear seconds later. Every instinct screamed at me to run. An eerie squeal escaped it as it charged toward me.

An adrenaline rush jolted me forward, fleeing whatever was chasing me. My eyes flicked over my shoulder. In the dense forest, the creature closed in on me. My screams pierced the air as I ran toward the entrance. Vines climbed down from the trees and twisted a tangled web over the opening, blocking my way out.

When I launched my orb into the cluster, it burst into flames, devouring the vines. The thorns, once menacing and thick, shriveled and turned to ash. The branches shrank away from the opening and cleared the path, enabling me to flee. I escaped as a thundering howl echoed through the forest.

My eyes were fixed on the grass meadows just past the entrance as I ran. I tripped and fell face first into their soft blanket of greenery, breaking my stride. On my hands and knees, I scrambled forward several feet before flipping around to view the forest. I sat still, my chest heaving and my breath racing. Only the broken orb had followed me out.

It lit up the sky with a brilliant ray of dazzling gold as it reconstructed itself. The orb slowly fell, landing in my palm. The sudden surge of power shook me. I closed my fist around it, feeling its warmth and energy radiating through me as it slowly orbited around me. The orb glowed brighter in approval as it hovered at my side, awaiting its next task. I felt a deep connection to the mysterious object. I knew it would be my companion and protector for as long as I needed it.

Once again, I entered the forest, my gaze alert. The orb floated in front of me, leading the way with its golden beam of light. A yellowish sheen spread over the forest, uncovering its secrets. The stench of death hung thick in the breezeless air, and the only sound that reached my ears was the damp dirt beneath my shoes. The forest's wild blossoms and thorny vines coiled around trees and dotted the forest floor, obscuring the shock of the scattered decay of human bones. In a haunting, beautiful way, it resembled the brushstrokes of a mad artist. The forest seemed to be the final resting place of some long-forgotten tragedy, but the truth was only known to the trees. I slowly moved forward, feeling I had stumbled upon something never meant to be seen.

As the entrance vanished behind me, I became submerged in the thick, towering trees. The damp dirt morphed into a soft blanket of moss, and the smell of death was replaced with a delicate bouquet of dried sage. The eerie feeling of being watched made my skin crawl. I slowly turned around. A horde of ghostly figures blocked the path, blurring the line between reality and nightmare. I lost my survival instinct as I ran for my life.

In the distance, my orb's fiery light flickered as I raced toward it, hoping it had found a way to escape. As it hovered over the woods edge of a flowing stream, I skidded to a halt. The stream repelled the shadow people, and they vanished into the thick mist surrounding the water. After several minutes, my orb urged me forward, and we continued our journey.

I seemed to be the only mortal alive within the forest walls. The intertwined branches formed a canopy of spiderwebs above me. The deeper I went, the more the trees morphed into hideous and threatening creatures. Their sharp twigs swooped down from the canopy or darted out of the dirt path, jutting toward me. A scream rose in my throat, but I didn't dare make a sound. Even though the forest threatened me, I had to keep moving.

My orb flashed bright light on a figure hidden in trees. I squinted and looked closer. It wasn't the shadow people. It was a woman. As she approached me, her long flowing dress dragged along the ground behind her. A bun of blonde hair adorned her head, and her mint-green eyes stared at me for what seemed like an eternity before she spoke. "I am the Guardian of the Woods. I protect the trees, and I am the keeper of the secrets of the forest. Three riddles await you. Only those who correctly answer the riddles will be allowed to proceed. Those who fail will be sent away. Good luck."

My brows furrowed in confusion as I stared at her, trying to process her words. "Isn't this the Dead Forest? Am I in the wrong place?"

"You are standing in the Dead Forest. Where I am standing is The Woods, but you must answer the riddles to enter."

"No one said anything about any riddles. I don't have time for games. How can I reach the Cave of Ashes?"

The Guardian's stance was unyielding. "Pass my test and you may enter my woods to continue to the Cave of Ashes. Fail, and you will never reach it."

"You can't be serious."

"I am serious." The Guardian's gaze intensified. "Now, choose wisely, for your fate is in your hands."

She stood her ground without fear of intimidation and wasn't going to let a person like me shake her resolve. As much as I was terrible at guessing riddles, I couldn't admit defeat. I had to outsmart her. As I peered over her shoulder, I decided to try a different approach. Maybe I could run past her. Without wasting any time, I bolted forward, hoping to outwit the puzzles that lay ahead. I slammed into an invisible barrier with her laughter echoing in my ears. The force of impact sent me tumbling backward.

Her eyes sparkled with amusement as she said, "The riddles cannot be outrun."

My frustration grew as I brushed dirt from my jeans and rose to my feet. "How many tries will I get?"

"There are no second chances. You must answer correctly the first time."

With confidence, I squared my shoulders, yet knowing that I had a slim chance of answering any of them correctly. I slowly exhaled, gathering my courage and steeling my nerves. I closed my eyes, concentrating on the task at hand. Upon opening my eyes, I said, "Hit me with the first riddle."

"Step back, Raven. Let the pros handle this." Caleb's voice hit my right ear.

As I spun around, I saw Caleb, Jaffa, and Eve. Standing behind them were my aunt, my brother, Hathor, Hypatia, and Rick. I opened my mouth to speak, but no words came out. I was overwhelmed by the sight of them all standing there, and my eyes filled with tears.

"Surprise!" Caleb shouted, raising his hands. My orb hovered near him. "Go away, pesky firefly," he said with sarcasm and shooed it away.

My orb returned to my side and sat on my shoulder.

Horus placed his hand on his chest, declaring, "We couldn't let you embark on this mission alone. Together, we must face these dangers."

Jaffa shoved him aside. "Lies. Your safety is relative to him and the others. It is their own agenda that has brought them here."

It didn't matter why they came. With them by my side, I was no longer the sole warrior in this fight. With their combined strength and power, we could surely defeat the witch, but then I remembered Eve's and Jaffa's warnings. *If your goal is to kill everyone, then follow Raven. If you want them to live, then stay here. The more of you who insist on going, the more Raven and the task are put at risk.* "What about the warning?" I asked, directing my question to Eve and Jaffa. "You both said that the risk increased as more people joined."

"A vision appeared to me," Eve said. "Though Jaffa managed to unlock more of your magic, my vision showed you are not powerful enough to stop the witch on your own. In light of this, we made the decision to follow you."

Jaffa pursed her lips tightly as she assessed the Guardian. "It appears our wits will also be put to the test."

A smug expression graced Caleb's face as he replied, "You can test my wits all you want. But you won't find me lacking. My abilities are impeccable and I am sharp as a tack."

"Each person before me will be given three riddles to answer. You may go first if you like."

"Look Wood, we don't have time for games. One list of riddles for the group."

"I also said I didn't have time for games too," I replied. "That didn't matter."

The Guardian shook her head. "No one will pass without answering the riddles."

After pushing her way to the front, Jaffa leveled her gaze on the Guardian. The Guardian mirrored Jaffa's scowl. They were locked in a glare standoff. Who would be the first to look away? As Jaffa summoned her arsenal of flames, her eyes never strayed from the Guardian. "Either recite three riddles, and only three riddles, or I'll set your beloved woods on fire," she vowed.

Applause erupted from Caleb. "Brutal. I love it."

Jaffa's gaze remained fixed on the Guardian as she ignored him. The Guardian's gaze briefly shifted to the many trees towering around her before she circled back to Jaffa. The corners of her lips curled upward into a nasty snarl. "Very well, demon. I will present the first riddle. Lives without a body, hears without ears, speaks without a mouth, to which the air alone gives birth. What am I?"

I rolled my eyes and sighed. What the hell was that? I didn't see why people enjoyed riddles so much. It seemed like a waste of time to me. Our focus should be on defeating the witch, not solving riddles. Time was running out, and a solution was needed. We needed to brainstorm ideas instead of answering annoying riddles. Wait. Could we use the Guardian to our advantage?

Caleb snapped his fingers and blurted, "An echo."

Her face held no expression as she replied, "Correct."

Caleb brought his fisted into his chest and boasted, "I knew it."

"I will present the second riddle. I never was, am always to be. No one ever saw me, nor ever will. And yet I am the confidence of all to live and breathe on this terrestrial ball. What am I?"

Rick stepped forward, a huff rattling his lips. "Ha! That's an easy one. "Tomorrow."

Again, she calmly stated, "Correct."

Caleb and Rick high-fived each other.

"I will present the third and final riddle. "What am I?"

Rick and Caleb shook their heads as they stared at one another. Everyone was in deep thought, considering the riddle's implications, as nobody wanted to risk giving the wrong answer. The riddle was three simple words, but not so straightforward. Was the question about her or just in general? Maybe it was a trick? Because if we answered incorrectly, we were out. I closed my eyes and let the words fill my mind. What...am...I? The answer hit me like a lightning bolt, and my eyes shot open. I raised my hand and said, "I think I know the answer."

Caleb's eyes burned into mine. "You think you know?"

"Let her answer," the Guardian ordered.

I stood before the Guardian and took a deep breath before answering. With confidence in my voice, I said, "A question."

The Guardian bowed and stepped aside as she smiled for the first time. A cool breeze blew through the entrance, rustling leaves. It dawned on me that I had answered correctly and we had been granted permission to enter the Woods.

Chapter 10

As we followed the Guardian into her woods, a similar eerie darkness surrounded us, like a void swallowing everything in its entirety. The bouquet of dried sage was once again replaced by damp earth, but there were no signs of the shadow people. What was the Guardian doing to prevent the fear-provoking creatures from soiling her woods? I glanced at her. She looked primitive in the hair and clothes she wore, as if she were from another era. I wondered how long she had been stuck in these woods. Her confident strides indicated authority, and I assumed that the Guardian was the only thing that kept the shadow people away. My curiosity piqued, and I asked, "I'm sorry, I don't mean to pry. How long have you lived here?"

"I belong to the trees and earth." Her words emitted power. "I have lived here as long as they have."

My jaw dropped. Despite appearing human, she was not. "What are you?" I asked.

A sigh filled the air as my aunt shooed me away. "Manners, Raven."

Laughing softly, the Guardian answered, "It's okay. She's allowed to be curious. I'm a dryad, a nature spirit. I was born from trees."

A million questions flooded my mind, but I remained silent as I stared in awe. I had never seen a creature like her. A short time ago, there were no vampires, vampire gods, fire demons, or dryads in my world. I had no idea my bloodline traced back to vampire gods or that the woman who gave birth to me was a witch, let alone a witch killer. As I tried to make sense of it all, one thing was certain: my life had become more complicated. This realization heightened both my determination and fear. What if this was just a dream and I suddenly woke up?

As he pinched my arm, Caleb mocked, "It's not a dream."

The sting confirmed its reality, and I pushed him away. "What's wrong with you?"

"Just proving you're awake."

"That's not how to prove someone is awake; that's how to prove someone is an ass."

A smirk spread across his face as he shrugged. "It worked, didn't it?"

I sneered at him. "You're so annoying."

"I think we've already come to that conclusion once before."

"Enough," Hathor said as she flipped her blonde locks over her shoulder. "We should be focusing on the witch and the return of our people. As Eve concluded, Raven isn't strong enough to stop her. The ancestors have absolutely been of no help. Therefore it is up to us. We must pool our power and come at her as one force."

"I'm sure that's what the others thought," Rick pointed out, "before she snatched them up and abducted them."

"Well, do you have a better idea?" Hathor asked, with irritation lacing her tone.

Hypatia came to her partner's defense. "He's merely pointing out the obvious. Something you failed to see."

Horus flexed his muscles. "She will not get past me."

The witch wouldn't be defeated by bickering or pride. Hathor was right. We had to come together if we were to succeed. Without unity, we would fail. I turned to the Guardian and asked, "Since the only way into the Cave of Ashes is through your woods, you must have seen the witch and her victims. We have come a long way to save them and destroy her, but we need to act quickly. Can you provide any information that might help us? And how did she get past you without answering the riddles?"

"The trees whispered of shrouded figures. Sunlight fled the woods upon their arrival and has yet to return. Even the air was filled with dread that could not be explained. I cannot say whether one of them was the witch you speak of; however, the terror emanating from the trees was quite profound." She looked directly at me as she said, "She did not pass by me."

What was the explanation for the sun's disappearance, and how did the witch escape the riddles? Was the witch responsible for the sudden darkness? Was she protecting her vampire captives from the burning rays? But why had the sun not returned? Was that on purpose—like she knew we were coming? Maybe it was a trap, and she was baiting us? We had to determine if the witch was behind the sun's disappearance, and if so, why. We also had to understand how she made it past the Guardian. Until we knew, we couldn't approach the Cave of Ashes. Our only hope of saving the vampires, and Brandon, was uncovering the truth.

Eve and I both blurted at the same time, "Something's not quite right."

"If the witch banished the sun to bring vampires into the forest," Eve continued before I could, "then why keep it banished once they were in the cave?" Eve answered her own question. "She knew more would come—us. They're not hostages, they're bait, to lure us. She's preparing for a fight. We cannot afford to be caught off guard."

"And how did she escape the riddles?" I added, but no one responded. Their focus was the vanishing sun.

"A battle is what she deserves. If she wants one, then I'll give it to her," Horus said, puffing out his chest and clenching his fists.

He was a hothead, and a thousand times stronger than me, but he needed to lower his confidence level and get off his high horse. She probably counted on him storming the castle, but he'd fall right into her plan and put everyone in danger. No one would call him out, so I did. "That kind of attitude will get us killed."

As his cold eyes burned a hole in my soul, he curled his lips and bared his fangs at me. I stuck my hand in his face and stopped him before he could speak. "Don't you think our parents and the Council did the same thing? If they couldn't protect themselves from her magic, why should you think you can?"

"That was epic, Raven." Caleb pointed at Horus. "You wiped the smirk right off his smug face." He acknowledged me with a curt nod. "Not to mention your speculation is spot-on."

The unexpected compliment made me blush. A smile tugged at the corners of my lips as I stammered, "Thank you."

"If she has indeed set a trap, we would be fools to enter the cave." Jaffa pointed out, hanging gloom over our heads once more. "We need the element of surprise. We must turn the tables on her."

She was right, but how could we accomplish it? Closing my eyes, I tuned out the noise around me and focused on my thoughts. I knew the witch was strong and clever and had outwitted all of us before, and somehow the Guardian too. I had to come up with a daring and innovative plan. The idea of using my own body as bait to lure the witch away was completely unconventional. I was willing to take the risk to save everyone, and I knew that if I could distract her, it would give my allies the opportunity to free my parents and give me the power I needed to finish the job. "What if I use myself as bait?"

"A brave but a foolish act," Horus said, giving his two cents.

My aunt crossed her arms as she rejected my plan. "My answer is no. It's too dangerous."

"Agreed. It's too risky. There must be a better way. How about the ancestors? Our communication with them was cut short by the witch's entrance. It might be a good idea to contact them again and seek their advice," Caleb suggested.

My ruse was a bit crazy, so I understood their perspective. If I caught her off guard, I could profit from her confusion. However, Caleb had a valid point regarding contacting the ancestors. Their knowledge of the witch was greater than ours. "I think my plan will give us the upper hand, but Caleb makes a valid point. Perhaps we should summon the ancestors."

"They have not helped so far," Hathor pointed out. "They should have had more control over their host."

"Could we use a decoy to pose as Raven?" Jaffa suggested. "Surely there is a spell that can make someone appear as someone else?"

"I'll do it," Horus volunteered. "Then, once the witch gets close enough, I rip out her heart. She won't see it coming."

The mere thought of murder sent a chill down my spine, and my stomach twisted in protest. Even just the idea of murder seemed too horrifying to comprehend. All we had to do was stop her plans, whatever they may be. I could not take a life, no matter how dire the circumstances were. The vampire god believed himself above all others, but even vampires must have a code of conduct to live by. As I found my voice, I said, "We aren't killing her!" I had to make him understand the consequences of his actions and convince him murder wasn't the answer.

Gritting his teeth, he looked at me, his eyes burning with anger. "She must be punished for her crimes."

As my aunt rested her hand on his shoulder, she said, "That is a matter for the Council."

"I am just a bystander listening in," the Guardian interjected, "but a witch powerful enough to adduct gods, omit the sun, and bypass the riddles will have knowledge of the past, present, and future. Is this lineage of ancestors the original witches?"

"Yes," Eve replied.

"What is their relationship with this witch?"

"In short, the ancestors used godly DNA to create a child. Raven is that child," Eve explained. "A surrogate was needed to carry the child to term. Their choice was the witch, and she betrayed them."

The Guardian furrowed her brow and pursed her lips in a thin line. When she spoke, her voice was authoritative and stern. "The original witches were cunning and all-knowing. A mere witch would not have the power to deceive them. They would have known everything about her before they agreed to have her carry this child. Betrayal would not have surprised them. Whoever this witch is, and whatever she has done, the ancestors are involved."

Shock furrowed in everyone's brow. Were the ancestors the ones who betrayed us? If the ancestors had known about the witch's plans to kill me, why even create me? Why allow her to kill all those witches and steal their power? What was their plan for me—death? And what about Isis? Wasn't she their ruler? Wouldn't they have been terrified of her wrath for deceiving her? However, they weren't among the living. What punishment could she bring? If what the Guardian said was true, it changed everything, and none of any of that made sense.

"The witch was careless," the Guardian continued. "If she had intended to kill her hostages, why block out the sun? She also left it hidden, therefore, she knew more vampires would come after her. I feel she means no threat to her captives. You are right to assume she is using them as bait. What you are all planning to do, this witch is counting on. She wants Raven. You cannot send Raven into that cave. She is the last person who should approach the witch."

Jaffa broke the silence and disagreed. "The vampires and the human are unconscious, hanging from the roof of the cave. If she truly meant them no harm, why torture them this way?"

"Or you saw what she wanted you to see."

A nasty scowl twisted Jaffa's brow. "I am a demon. I plant seeds of deception, not the other way around."

"Hold up," Caleb said, spreading his arms between Jaffa and the Guardian. "We need to talk this thing through as none of us are quite certain what the hell is going on."

"Each person has a different flavor," Rick said, nodding.

Caleb agreed, "And none of it adds up."

"Your conclusion has some inconsistencies," Rick said to the Guardian. "For instance, Eve read the witch's thoughts. It was revealed to the witch by the ancestors that Raven's birthmarks contained a hidden code that would allow her to access her magic. When we confronted the ancestors, they denied making such a statement. Rather, they claimed Raven's magic had to be approved by Isis and Osiris, her parents, in order to access its full potential. And that's just the tip of the iceberg."

Caleb picked up where Rick left off. "A vampire named Nico threw a wrench into the witch's plans by walking in on her during labor. He watched the witch drink the baby's blood right in front of him. Nico grabbed the baby and fled just as the ancestors came in and apprehended the witch. It was the ancestors who imprisoned her for her betrayal, and somehow after nineteen years she broke free and has come after Raven."

Horus thrust himself into the conversation as he said, "And I read Raven's blood. Her magic must be awakened by our parents."

"This is true," Jaffa conveyed. "In spite of my efforts, I was unable to awaken all of Raven's magic. Her bloodline shut me out before I could fully achieve it."

A blank expression played across the Guardian's face as she listened to the conversation. Though the wheels in her mind seemed to be turning, she showed no visible signs of emotion. I, on the other hand, shuddered as an overwhelming surge of anxiety rippled through me. My brain could not keep up with all of these variations. How had my life become so complicated? It was all because of the ancestors' interference. If I managed to escape this situation alive, how would I explain it to my adoptive parents, and would I even be considered their daughter? I shook away all the uncertainties and focused on what needed to be done. We had to stop the witch.

The Guardian's response was directed at both Caleb and Rick, "There are also inconsistencies in your tale. Why did the ancestors create a child? Furthermore, how could the ancestors have been unaware that the imprisoned witch had escaped? I find it odd that they didn't reveal the threat the witch would cause."

"We don't know," Eve admitted. "We think the witch wanted Raven to be overpowered, robbed of her magic, and killed."

"What would she gain by killing Raven?"

Eve shrugged. "Power I assume."

"Quiet, everyone!" Hypatia ordered. "I heard something."

Hathor stared into the murkiness of the forest as she echoed, "I heard it too."

My orb's light shone on a person stumbling down the path. I recognized Brandon's sandy brown hair the moment it caught a ray of light. My chest ached as my lungs forgot how to breathe. The world narrowed down to just him and me as I ran toward him, barely believing he was real. Each step between us felt like an eternity.

"Raven, no!" Caleb and Horus yelled together, charging after me.

My pace slowed as I neared him and I called his name. Caleb and Horus were already beside him, along with the others. At the sight of his blood-soaked shirt, I broke into a cold sweat. As I gazed into Brandon's lifeless eyes, he collapsed into my arms. I didn't even have time to process what had happened before Caleb and Horus shoved me aside and kneeled beside him. I stood frozen as they fed him vampire blood.

Brandon's body jolted upright, and his eyelids fluttered open. He took a deep breath and rose to his feet, looking at me with a confused expression. He opened his mouth to speak, but the words caught in his trembling throat. He slowly reached out and touched my face, I think, to make sure I was real. Tears rolled down his cheeks as he said, "You're here," his voice barely above a whisper.

I hugged him tightly, and he buried his head in my shoulder. His warm tears ran down my neck, and I felt a rush of emotion as I embraced him. We stood there, holding each other before Caleb pulled us apart.

"What about the others?"

Rick waved Caleb away as he approached Brandon. A look of concern etched on his brow, as he asked, "What happened? Who did this to you, the witch?" Rick's gaze shifted to Brandon's fading bruises. "I'm so sorry," he whispered.

Brandon stared at Rick with wide eyes. A second later, he shouted, "Rick!" and hugged him. "There's no way. I can't believe you're here."

As Rick patted Brandon's back, he stared at him, asking, "Who did this to you?"

Brandon glanced around noticing the others, his eyes narrowing as they landed on Hypatia.

She nodded. "Brandon."

"Hypatia."

The coolness between them sparked my interest. What was going on there? Was Hypatia trouble? Not only was there tension between Hypatia and Hathor, but there was also tension between Brandon and Hypatia.

"And what about the others?" Caleb interrupted. "Were they injured as well?"

"I don't recall much," Brandon sighed, running his hands through his hair.

"What's the last thing you remember?" Rick asked.

"Um, waking up in a dark cave. I'm sure I wasn't alone. I heard groans. Then everything went black, and somehow ended up here."

"I can look inside his mind and see what he cannot recall," Jaffa offered, with a confident nod.

Rick gripped Brandon's shoulder and asked, "Are you game?"

"Of course."

After placing her fingertips on his temples, Jaffa slid her eyelids shut. Brandon stood still, his gaze fixed on something in the distance as if in a trance. His arms hung loose at his sides and his muscles relaxed. There didn't seem to be pain as with me when Jaffa read his mind.

Her eyes opened moments later. "The others are still unconscious," she declared. "Brandon was released to lure us back to the cave. The trees caused Brandon's injuries."

A frown spread across Brandon's brow. "Since when do trees attack?"

Jaffa's statement didn't faze the Guardian, who shrugged her shoulders and said, "Perhaps the witch spelled them."

"They're pretty aggressive," I said, adding my two cents. "They tried to attack me, too."

"What difference does any of this make?" Hathor snapped, daring anyone to challenge her. "We need to focus on our rescue attempt and not get distracted."

"And who are you?" Brandon asked.

"I'm the one trying to save the day," Hathor said, her eyes burning.

"Brandon, this is Hathor, Kohath's maker, and a member of the Ten," Rick said and gestured to my aunt and brother. "That's Nephthys, Isis's sister, and also a member of the Ten. And that's Horus, Isis and Osiris's son, and a member of the Ten."

Brandon nodded. "I get it. You're all invested. They've got your people."

With his fists clenched, Horus vowed, "I won't rest until I get them back."

My magical orb nudged my shoulder as it spun around me. I shooed it away.

"What the hell is that?" Brandon blurted out.

"Don't worry. It's annoying but harmless," Caleb said, before turning back to my orb and muttering a few choice words.

It charged toward Caleb before rushing back to me and nudging me again. I petted the orb with my hand. "It's okay, little guy. We're family now." I extended my hands, and it landed inside my palms. Its energy radiated through me as a brilliant array of colors swirled upward, surrounding me. A tingle of excitement rushed up my throat as I realized it was trying to communicate with me. I took a deep breath, closed my eyes, and concentrated. Letters flooded my mind as they formed words and sentences. *Secrets remain hidden. The ancestors hold the key to defeating the witch. Summon the ancestors.* I gasped and stepped back, my heart racing. "How am I supposed to do that?" I whispered.

My aunt put her hand on my shoulder and asked, "Do what, Raven?"

I pressed my lips together as I turned to face her and attempted to keep that news to myself. If I didn't tell them, they'd just read my thoughts, but how could I summon them? I wasn't my mother. I lacked the power of my mother. Although they would expect me to, I feared disappointing them. I stared at my aunt as I confessed, "My orb told me the ancestors would be the key to defeating the witch and I must summon them."

"This mess changes every minute," Caleb groaned.

She ignored him. I was her focus. "What proof did the orb provide?"

The Guardian spoke before I could respond. "I agree with the orb. It makes more sense. The ancestors are all-knowing. They must enter the Cave of Ashes. They imprisoned the witch before, so why couldn't they do it again?"

After Eve approached me, Jaffa followed. The two stood before me, staring. Jaffa spoke first. "We need to summon them, right?" she asked.

I nodded in agreement.

Eve's gaze flickered between Jaffa and me. "We can do it together."

"As a magical being, I can strengthen the summons," the Guardian said.

"We might not be able to equal Isis's power, but together we should be able to summon the ancestors," Eve concluded.

Chapter 11

As before, a row of seven ancestors stood in front of us, their physical forms flickering like holograms. Their expressions were perfectly still, as if carved from stone, giving no clue as to what was going on in their minds. Their instantaneous appearance was eerie and unsettling. Had they anticipated our summons? Their gaze shifted from me to the others as they approached us.

In a stare-down standoff, each side refused to speak. Eve broke the ice. "It is time to hear the truth." Her tone was clear and direct.

The suspense grew, and anxiety coursed through me. I felt helpless, on edge, and powerless to change what was about to happen. I prayed for good news, although I braced myself for the worst.

"We have come forward to correct our wrongs," the ancestor said as he stepped forward, his face shrouded by a hooded cloak.

Was I just another error they needed to fix? The thought gnawed at me, filling me with unease. I couldn't help but wonder if my entire existence was a problem they were trying to solve.

"Our seers predicted a future in which the Dark Spirits destroyed the world, annihilating our lineage. Such destruction could not be tolerated. Immediate action was crucial before the Dark Spirits could complete their rampage. A tribrid child would be created. The child would possess the power, fairness, and compassion of magic, godliness, and humanity. The child would restore our human forms and make us immortal. As a result, we would rule over all supernatural beings, preventing the Dark

Spirits' massacre. Unbeknownst to us, the Dark Spirits had deceived our seers. The vision was fabricated."

Confusion crept into my brain, overwhelming me. Dark Spirits? Annihilation? There were so many versions, I couldn't keep up. What was the truth? Was there no way out of the nightmare I was living? I paused and took a deep breath. The facts had to be my focus, and I had to make my decisions based on logic and reason, not fear.

He continued, shattering my thoughts. "The tribrid child is Raven. Her birth revealed the truth of the Dark Spirits' deception. Despite her innocence, she was the key to our demise and the Dark Spirits' success. Knowing the full potential of Raven's power, the Dark Spirits devised a plan to acquire it. By sacrificing Raven, they could gain her abilities and use them for their day of reckoning and gain control over the supernatural world."

His words made my stomach clench. How many beings were plotting my destruction? I was powerless in the face of such dominating forces. Fear gripped my heart, knowing that my options were either to fight or die.

"We immediately captured Raven's surrogate host and the Dark Spirits, but as you are all aware, they eventually escaped. The witch murders began, and we knew the host was responsible. We feared that if the truth was revealed, the Dark Spirits could easily track down Raven and use their magic to overtake her. The purpose of our silence was to protect her."

"You want me to bring you back to life after you have affected so many lives: vampires, gods, witches, and humans. It's not happening." I clenched my fists and shouted, "I won't do it. You can remain dead for all I care." I didn't give anyone a chance to reply as I whispered, "Transform my physical form into a dream, and my whereabouts unseen."

I vanished from their sight and appeared alone on the pathway. My orb had slipped my mind. How would it find me? Could it be summoned? However, its bright light would make my location obvious to others. In a "whatever" gesture, I flapped my hand in the air and continued on my way.

Cold air nipped at my skin as I walked through the dark woods. I wasn't sure whether it was day or night. I didn't have the moon or sunlight to guide me, only the whispers of the trees. Would the trees betray me and reveal my location to the Guardian? Their loyalty to her extended far beyond a mere witch trespassing through their woods. I paused, listening for any signs that would indicate I was being followed. Silence met my ears. I carefully moved forward, making my way further down the path and possibly toward the Cave of Ashes, determined to uncover its location.

The deeper I delved into the woods, the shallower my breath became. An aura of strength enveloped me, raising my pulse with every step. An electric charge filled the air, and I knew something was about to happen. Could it be the Cave of the Ashes? Was I close? The hairs on my arms rose as I followed the powerful, magical pull down the path. I turned the corner, and suddenly found myself standing before the opening of a cave. Its entrance was hidden in the shadows, but the air outside the cave was dense and heavy, filled with an ancient energy. Cave of Ashes!

A strong arm pulled me backward, and I spun to see Caleb standing there glaring at me. "Are you insane? Have you got a death wish?" he demanded.

I stared at him in disbelief. How did he find me? The look on his face chilled me to the bone. He was fuming.

Rage emanated from him as he grabbed me by the shoulders. "What the hell were you thinking?" He stepped back after letting go of my shoulders and let out an exasperated groan.

I forced words out of my bone-dry mouth. "I just wanted to get away from everyone and everything."

"I understand. You're only 19, and you've already got a price tag on your head. The ancestors made some serious mistakes, but they imprisoned the witch and the Dark Spirits once before. They can do it again." He gestured the other way with his hand. "Come back with me. Hear them out. They want to set things right, and the only way to do that is by defeating the witch and the Dark Spirits."

As I contemplated my response, my orb's brilliant glow whizzed past me. After gently nudging me, it snuggled up to me like a cat. "I'm glad to see you, too," I said.

Within seconds, the temperature dropped. An electric charge shot through my body as "danger" flashed through my brain. In the darkness of the cave, something moved. My eyes darted around, searching for whatever it was. I knew I had to run, and fast.

Caleb's tone grew tense as he asked, "What's wrong?"

"There's something in—" My voice was cut off by a pair of boney hands gripping my throat and yanking me into the cave. I gasped for air and thrust an elbow into my attacker.

"Raven!" Caleb's shout met my ears just before the cave's entrance collapsed, trapping me inside with whatever held me.

The glow of my orb caught my attention. The iridescent ball of light floating in the air was an obvious target. In secret, I shooed it away, fearing the thing would destroy it. In the cave's roof, it hid itself among jagged rocks.

My calm demeanor prevented the thing's claws from digging deeper into my neck. A short time ago, I would have been terrified out of my mind and pushed the panic button. The last few months had changed me. My life had suddenly been infiltrated by darkness, as well as vampires, gods, and witches. But what sort of thing was this? A witch's minions, a cave creature, or a Dark Spirit? In this mutating nightmare, I was its prize, and my goal was to survive and find a way out.

It dropped me next to a pile of boulders and loomed over me. As my gaze darted upward, I came face-to-face with its grayish skull and sunken glowing eyes. Gasping, I scrambled backward on my hands and knees. There were hundreds of veins spiraling through its head and morphing into tentacles and scales on its body. It tilted its skull down at me, watching me like a bug under a microscope. Slowly getting up, I asked, "What do you want?"

The creature said nothing, but a thin tendril shot out of its body and floated toward me. I shuddered and shrank away. A twisted grin spread across the monster's gaunt ashen lips, revealing stained and jagged fangs. Retracting its tendril, it hissed, "Blood bending with you will be a pleasure."

My eyes scanned the area for weapons, but nothing caught my attention. My only chance of escaping was outsmarting the creature with my magic. Looking into its eyes, I asked, "Where is the witch?"

In a low growl, it replied, "The witch served her purpose."

My breath caught in my throat. Had it killed her or was it lying to throw me off guard? As far as I could tell, the cave was void of any human life. Where were the others? Had they been killed along with the witch? The clock was ticking, and I had to think fast to come up with a plan, but my only option was to uncover the truth. My voice quivered as I asked, "What have you done to the witch, to the others?"

Again, it grinned at me as it answered, "You'll find out soon enough." The creature lunged forward and clawed at me. Its razor-sharp talons pierced through my clothing and left deep gashes on my skin. The creature's eyes were filled with rage and insanity, and its growl sounded like a mixture between a wild animal and a possessed demon.

A rock caught my foot as I backed away. I hit the ground hard, sucking air from my lungs. The creature pounced on top of me, its claws outstretched, its eyes cold with malice. In a single breath, I commanded my magic. "Ignite!" I cried. A pillar of fire erupted from my hand, bathing the creature in searing heat. Smoke hissed from its scale-covered skin as it screamed and stumbled back.

An adrenaline rush pushed me to my feet. Despite all odds, I won. As I raised my fist in celebration, I heard a noise behind me. When I turned around, a clawed fist slammed against my temple and crumpled me to the ground. A warm and wet sensation spread through my hair and dripped down my face. The smell of blood traveled up my nostrils as I struggled to remain conscious. A second creature emerged and the pair hovered over me, one of which I had burned, and the other much smaller. They appeared to be communicating, but their language was foreign to me. They burst out with malicious laughter. The shrill sound pierced my ears. As I slipped into unconsciousness, the horror around me faded.

A sharp sting in my arms roused me from my unconscious state. My eyes fluttered open to blurred images surroundings me. It took several seconds for my vision to clear. In the haze, I sat propped up on the rocks, my hands and feet bound with ropes. A dreadful feeling gripped me as my own blood flowed through translucent tubes into the creatures' grotesque bodies. Fear jolted me wide awake. *Was this blood bending?* The creatures' eyes glowed with venom, and a satisfied hiss escaped their lips. I struggled to break free, but the ropes around my hands and feet coiled tighter. The power of my magic would free me. My mind immediately sprang into action to cast a spell of extermination. "Two plus one, equals three. Drink my blood, and I will poison thee."

Stumbling backwards, the creatures tore the tubes from their arms. One by one, their tentacles withered away, revealing decayed flesh. As they fled my blood, their scaly bodies weakened and collapsed. Green slime oozed from their eye sockets as their bodies crumbled to dust, leaving the only trace of their existence.

A magical blast crackled through the air, sending rope fibers flying in all directions. Some caught fire and disintegrated in midair while others fell softly, like charred snowflakes, onto the blackened ground around me. My breath caught in my throat as I realized I was no longer bound.

The cave echoed with a whirling noise. As I turned, I gasped in delight as my orb landed in my hands. Its familiar glow filled me with clarity and purpose, and I declared, "It's time to find my others."

A faint hum emitted from the orb's surface as it whizzed forward, stopped, and spun around to face me. A variety of colors shimmered from its surface as it hovered in the air, waiting for me. It gently nudged my shoulder and moved forward a couple of inches. "Do you want me to follow you?" It bounced up and down as it glowed brightly. I quickened my pace to keep up with my orb and followed it through a winding, moss-covered passage, leading us deeper into the cave.

My orb stopped at a narrow opening surrounded by jagged rocks. I paused, uncertain of what lay ahead, when the orb entered and beckoned me to follow. In the dark cave, my hair stood on end as my orb's light illuminated the back corner. The ceiling was covered with giant cocoons. There was something inside them. Stepping closer, I squinted up at them. I gasped out loud when my orb shone its light on them. The cocoons contained my parents, the Council, and Margarete. The witch lay sickeningly pale on the ground beneath them, curled up in a fetal position. Deep gashes covered her arms and legs. A sense of horror and grief coursed through me as I stared at her bloody clothes.

I leaned over the witch, listening. Shallow breath sounds met my ear. She was still alive! Hesitantly, I nudged her shoulder. No response. I nudged harder. Her eyelashes fluttered open after a few seconds. The look of sorrow and regret played across her face. Tears spilled from her eyes as she stared at me. "I'm sorry," she whispered. "They controlled me, my actions. I would never hurt anyone."

Studying her face and eyes, I realized the madness was gone, replaced by remorse. "What happened to you? Who did this?" I asked.

"The Dark Spirits took over my soul shortly before I gave birth to you. I was trapped inside my own body for nineteen years and I couldn't call out for help. Not even my magic could save me. As I watched the destruction I caused, the death I caused, I was horrified. All they wanted was you, your power, and I helped them find you. I was their pawn, and in the end, they drained my blood too, and then set me free and left me here to die."

As I squeezed her hand, I told her, "You don't have to die. My parents or the Council can give you blood."

She glanced toward the cocoons and sighed. "They will not help me."

"Did you put them in these cocoons?"

She nodded.

"Let them go, and I promise you they will heal you."

Her body shuddered as more tears fell from her eyes. "Why would you do that?"

"It was never my intention to kill you, but rather to stop you from killing others. Whatever is in this cave with us is far too powerful. I killed two creatures, but I suspect they are only the beginning. I need all of my power to fight, which my parents must approve of. I will ensure they heal you, but you must agree to release them from these cocoons. If you don't, we will all die. You must do this." Her gaze held mine, but she remained silent. My apprehension grew as I awaited her response.

A sob escaped her throat, and her gaze shifted to the floor. She shook her head slowly, conveying her reluctance with her expression.

"Please! Please!" I begged.

In a weakened voice, she recited, "Incantatio frangatur, Lamia tuto rediit, Praesens restauratum, praeteritum congelatum, A vampire confirmatus est."

Although I didn't understand the language, the word vampire immediately caught my attention. The cocoons crashed and scattered dust everywhere as they tumbled to the ground with a thunderous roar. My parents, Margarete, and the Council members appeared with a burst of air. My mother stepped forward, her eyes locked on the witch and her voice teeming with anger. "You will never use my daughter's blood for your own gain. I will not allow it."

I shook my head and held her back, explaining, "You don't understand. She's a victim. She needs *your* blood."

"Raven, get away from her," my father commanded.

"I will not. Give her your blood!" I shouted, clenching my fists. "She's dying. She's not a threat to me anymore. Heal her. She deserves a second chance."

"Why should we do this after everything she's done?" My father's gaze darted to the gashes on my arms and my head. "Who did this to you, her?"

"No, the cave creatures."

The witch's shaky voice filled my ears. "They are not cave creatures. They are Dark Spirits."

"Did I kill Dark Spirits? They looked like scaly, tentacled creatures to me."

"Yes." She shuddered and gasped for breath as her eyelids closed. Her head tilted to one side, and she fell unconscious.

"No," I screamed, spinning around to my parents. "Heal her! Don't let her die!"

Kohath rushed toward the witch, stabbed his wrist, and placed it over her mouth, allowing his blood to flow into her. His power radiated through her, transforming her pale skin and gray lips into a beautiful rosy glow. Seeing her eyes open again, he let go and stepped back.

She glanced at me before her gaze found Kohath. An expression of gratitude lit up her face. "Thank you for saving my life."

"I did so for Raven. I would not have been so kind."

Relief flooded from my lungs as said, "Yes, thank you," before glaring at my parents. "They should have helped you and me."

"Why do you care about her?" my father asked.

"Because she's a victim just like all of us. She told me she had no control over her actions. She was powerless to resist their evil. After she served her purpose, the Dark Spirits drained her blood and left her for dead."

His eyes narrowed in disapproval, and I could see the frustration etched into his forehead. "Raven, you can't believe everything someone tells you. I think there's more to the story than just her being a pawn in some supernatural game."

I narrowed my eyes, hoping to convey a look of defiance. He was just a bystander, and he had no right to judge me. I was in control and determined to make my own decisions. "Father, I'm not gullible. You haven't been around my whole life. I have my own opinions and make my own decisions. I must stand up for what I believe in. You don't know me well enough to judge me," I repeated, emphasizing my point.

He opened his mouth to respond, but my mother veered in front of him and cut him off. "Osiris, don't you see the resemblance?" She tucked a strand of my hair behind my ear. "She's me when I was younger, compassionate, self-assured, and wanting to save the world."

He tilted his head, studying me. "And rather strong-willed I might add."

My mother never took her eyes off me. She took in all my features, perhaps comparing them to her own. The smile in her eyes sparkled with admiration as she seemed to look directly inside me, as if she saw something no one else could. Her heart pounded against mine as she held me tightly in her embrace. At that moment, I knew she loved me.

As she released me, she placed her fingertips on my temples, her eyes shining brightly. Her touch was gentle and soothing, sending warmth throughout my body. "Your magical powers have been granted."

With a deep breath, I remembered Jaffa's brutal attack, but my mother's touch brought my magic to life without hurting me. My body erupted with power, awakening dormant magic. My birthmarks slowly faded, transforming into golden hues that lit up the room. The world opened up to me in a way I had never imagined possible. As my magic soared through the air, my body transformed from a mere human into a vessel of extraordinary power. "Thank you, Mother," I whispered.

She smiled, her eyes twinkling with delight. "You're welcome, Raven."

Kohath quickly approached and gestured toward dark fog obscuring the pathway. He kept his voice low as he said, "We have company."

Shapes emerged from the darkness, and my heart beat faster as I recognized the Dark spirits. Invoking fireballs into the palms of my hands, I flung them into the fog, illuminating the creatures. The Dark Spirits scattered like cowards, and I emerged victorious. Despite my smugness, the ground rumbled under my feet, splitting open and engulfing a Council member. His shrill scream pierced my ears. My jaw dropped in horror as I watched the ground swallow him whole.

A series of shrieks echoed throughout the cave as the vampires called out one name. "Samuel!" Speeding toward the hole and digging up the earth, they uncovered his lifeless body. Kohath punctured his wrist, forced open Samuel's mouth, and offered his blood. As the droplets hit Samuel's tongue, he latched onto Kohath's wrist, and drank with greed. He rose to his feet moments later, and his comrades rejoiced and cheered him on.

A series of tremors rattled the cave, leaving deep cracks in the walls. Huge chunks of rock crumbled and fell to the ground, spewing out a thick cloud of dust and rubble. The unstable ground shifted and heaved, causing everyone to lose their footing and collide with each other. Through the veil of dust, wiry tentacles emerged, lashing out at anything that crossed their path, igniting further chaos. Shouts of terror reverberated throughout the cave, blending with the hissing of the Dark Spirits.

In order to survive, we had to find a way out of the cave. Despite my own fear, I summoned my inner strength and used my power to repel the relentless attacks. Magical electricity rushed through my veins, shaking my body. My eyes closed and I concentrated on the energy, gathering it into a single thought. As my eyes flew open, I yelled, "Ancient strength and supreme power, I invoke thee. Invisible shields of brick and stone surround me. Become the walls that set us free."

In an explosion of light, an immense dome emerged from my spell and fell over us, separating us from the Dark Spirits. They cried out in rage as their tentacles lashed out at the dome. Upon impact, debris flew inside the dome as shockwaves broke through the earth, knocking us to the ground. Dust covered our bodies, and the air reeked of dirt. Their tentacles continued to strike the dome, shaking the earth around us. As they realized their attack was futile, their screams intensified, nonetheless they pulled back, leaving us alone but far from safe.

"We can't stay here for much longer," Samuel said, with panic lacing his voice.

My father pressed his hands downward and shook his head. "Stay calm. We'll find a way out. First we need to determine how to outwit them."

"It seems like they're pushing us farther and farther into the cave." One Council member pointed out.

Another asked, "What can we do?"

In response, Kohath said, "Let's think this through. We're powerful beings. Surely, we can come up with a plan that works."

I focused on Margarete and the witch. They, most likely, could unlock this mystery. Margarete understood the spirit world. She might provide insights into the Dark Spirits' motivations. In contrast, the witch was intimately familiar with the Dark Spirits, so she was well versed in how to defeat them and their capabilities. The real key to ending this nightmare was in the ancestors' hands. They knew how to contain the Dark Spirits. It was their knowledge that we needed to defeat the Dark Spirits.

"We need the ancestors. They would be able to defeat the Dark Spirits," I said, interrupting the many opinions. "But the Dark Spirits sealed off the cave, and everyone we need is in the forest."

"Who all is on the other side?" Margarete asked.

"Aside from the ancestors, there are Horus, Nephthys, Hathor, Caleb, Hypatia, Rick, Jaffa, Eve, and Brandon since the witch freed him. Oh, and the Guardian."

Margarete frowned. "The Guardian?"

"She safeguards the woods. Considering we are on our own right now, Kohath is right. We need to devise a plan to defeat the Dark Spirits. Any suggestions?"

"Yes, witch," my father directed his comment to her. "Tell us."

Her reddish-brown hair fluttered over her shoulders as she tilted her head toward him. "All of you keep calling me witch. I have a name. It's Luna."

"Fair enough, Luna. Please answer my daughter's question."

As she replied, her blue eyes darkened. "The Dark Spirits' only objective is to conquer and destroy the supernatural world. Raven's blood will give them the power to accomplish that. Afterward, humans will become their slaves." She paused, and added, "However, they are vulnerable to fire, and can be killed easily, but they quickly multiply. If you kill one, four more will appear."

Margarete agreed, "Regeneration seems to happen as a simple exchange of energy between spirits, which we are powerless to control. It would be like stopping the wind from blowing."

"Well, that sucks," I said, then cringed to think that my blood would harness the creation of an army of unstoppable monsters. I resolved to do everything I could to prevent such a disaster from happening. "Then we'll burn this cave to the ground, with all of them inside."

Chapter 12

"Have you forgotten *we're* inside this cave?" a Council member asked, arching his perfect brow.

I looked him straight in the eye and answered, "No, but I also haven't forgotten that we're trapped in this cave with *them*. We have no choice but to destroy the cave and burn these things."

"Burning the cave would be too extreme," my father said, vetoing my plan. "Fire is death to a vampire, Raven. You know that, right? We must seek another solution."

I certainly wasn't an expert when it came to vampires. A few months ago, they were just fictional characters in books and movies. I never imagined I'd actually meet one, much less find out my parents were gods turned vampire. None of that mattered, though. Getting out of this mess did. My voice rose with emotion as I said, "As of this moment, we have one goal: destroy the Dark Spirits. If we don't, we'll die!"

My mother wrapped her arm around me and said, "We will find another way."

"*Is* there another way?" one of the Council members asked.

Kohath directed his question to Athaliah. "Any ideas?"

"Blood is my medium," Athaliah flatly replied. "Without a sample of theirs, I cannot provide a solution."

"Perhaps the others will find a way to break into the cave and free us," Samuel speculated. "We should wait and see."

Did everyone think my idea was too risky, doubting my abilities to execute it? Though, I'd be the first to confess to being a novice, that shouldn't be an automatic dismissal of my magic. The whole point was for me to gain access so I could use it against the Dark Spirits, and especially now since they threatened us.

Caleb hadn't found a way in. Help was not coming, no matter how much Samuel wanted it to be so. Without the ancestors, my magic was the only way to protect us, and I let everyone know. "That's not likely going to happen," I argued. "Caleb wouldn't let anything stand in his way of protecting Margarete. He'd be here by now if he'd found a way in."

"But we don't know for sure," Samuel countered.

"Raven is right," Margarete said, taking my side. "Caleb would go to any lengths to reach me. I suspect the Dark Spirits must have prevented outside entry. We need to figure out a way to breach it."

"My way is the way." I turned to Luna. "Combine your magic with Margarete's spirit power and break through the cave opening. You can get everyone out while I use myself as bait to attract the Dark Spirits in the opposite direction. Once it's safe, I'll build a fire barrier to confine them and burn the cave. Then I'll escape and seal them in."

Again, my father disapproved. "You just acquired your magic and haven't performed such a powerful spell. What if it doesn't work, or more importantly, what if you hurt someone or yourself? I won't allow it. It's too dangerous."

It was not his place to judge. Until a few days ago, he didn't even know I existed. Although I'd been a witch my entire life, I had no idea why my magic didn't work. Now, with my understanding in hand, I refused to back down. "I don't need your permission," I said defiantly, then quickly cast my spell. "Bronze and gold, bring forth your light. Rings of fire, grant me your might. In my hands, you will grow tall and bright." As I spoke, a saffron blaze encircled me, surging with magical energy as it crackled and hissed, illuminating the cave with golden light. The flames surged as I thrust them forward with one hand. The fiery blaze separated and darted around my father. In a frozen state, he stared wide-eyed at the flames whooshing on either side of him.

"Raven!" my mother shrieked as she scrambled toward me.

My free hand unleashed binding magic upon my mother, trapping her. As she struggled to move, I watched her face contort in surprise. In that moment, I was everyone's focus, especially Kohath and Athaliah. Their recognition made me feel invincible, as if I could conquer any obstacle that arose. I stood tall, ready to face whatever came my way.

By slamming my hands on the ground, I extinguished the flames and broke the spells, freeing my parents. Kohath and Athaliah approached me, admiration gleaming in their eyes. "The powers you possess are vast," Kohath said. "Overpowering a vampire god is an impressive feat."

Athaliah nodded and agreed. "The likes of which I have never seen."

My focus shifted to my parents. Instead of being amazed, they scowled and pursed their lips. Their disappointment was evident.

A loud roar swept through the cave commanding my attention. The ground rumbled under my feet as Dark Spirits flooded the cave, whipping their tentacles at us.

"Luna, get everyone out of the cave. I'll hold them back," I shouted, summoning my rings of fire and hurling the crackling flames at the Dark Spirits. My orb hovered by me, and I shooed it toward Luna. "Go with Luna."

Luna's hands fluttered at her sides as she stared at me.

"Now, Luna!"

Dark Spirits shifted upward, spiraling over Luna and the vampires. She bolted forward, herding the vampires toward the cave entrance while my orb followed. With my magic, I twisted the scorching flames into ropes. Screams echoed throughout the cave as I flung burning twine directly at the Dark Spirits and lassoed them like cattle. As the blaze collided with the Dark Spirits, I tightened the rope, engulfing them completely. Amidst the fire, the Dark Spirits disintegrated, leaving heaps of charred remains scattered throughout the cave. I expected resistance, but none came, and a wave of relief washed over me. I annihilated the Dark Spirits and ended their reign of terror.

A loud roar erupted behind me, and Luna's warning echoed in my mind: *Kill one, and four more will appear.* When I turned around and saw the cave walls lined with Dark Spirits, my breath caught in my throat. Their cold, hollow eyes swept over me with an eerie, unblinking stare. My overconfidence left me powerless against them. The cave had to be destroyed.

The Dark Spirits charged forward in a blur. As their growls reverberated through the cave, I ascended into the air. Heat swirled in my hands as I chanted, "From flames to dust, I command you to combust." A firestorm erupted from my hands and cascaded down the cave walls, igniting everything in its path. Under the crackling flames, the Dark Spirits' bodies imploded inside the blaze, sealing their fate.

An explosion of firebombs ripped through the cave. As the rocks caught fire and tumbled down the path, their roar drowned out everything else. Sparks flew in all directions, lighting up the darkness with a menacing red glow. As I zigzagged through the falling rocks, the intense heat clouded my vision, blistered my skin, and left me gasping for air. Even though I fell and scraped my knees and hands against rough gravel, I kept running. My life depended on it.

When the cave's entrance and those on the other side fell into my sight, I cried out in relief.

"Run faster!" they shouted.

The earth quaked inside the cave and the roof crumbled around me, knocking me flat on my back. In a moment of panic, I spewed out the first spell that came to mind. "Guardians of flesh, blood, and bones. I invoke your shields to..."

Boulders fell on top of me and the ground collapsed, plunging me into darkness. As I sank, I heard a booming noise, and realized it was my own heartbeat. I had a choice: either give up and die or fight for my life. I chose to fight. My screams for help went unanswered. The earth slowly swallowed me up, and my last thought before passing out was, "I should have run faster."

****

When I opened my eyes, confusion washed over me. Why was it so dark? Why did it smell of dirt? My body was heavy and motionless as I regained a sense of my surroundings. It dawned on me that I was still trapped inside the cave. My eyes adjusted to the darkness. Boulders, rocks, and dirt hovered inches above my head and torso but pinned down my legs. When I attempted to lift my head, searing pain shot down my arms and legs, forcing me to scream. I shut my eyes tight, trying to block out the agony and confusion.

After some time, the pain subsided. In my mind, flashes of memories flooded in; Dark Spirits, fire, the cave collapsing and breaking my spell. How long had I been lying there? Were the others looking for me? I should have listened to my father's warning. I'd been too confident and failed. I'd refused to back down, and that decision sealed my fate. In the end, my pride cost me everything.

My hand touched something wet in the dirt beside my legs. As I lifted my hand to inspect the wet substance, excruciating spasms gripped my core. I was sure I was going to faint as tears streamed down my cheeks. I forced myself to take a few deep breaths as I glanced at my hand. My fingers were covered in blood! I was bleeding and alone, and I had no way out. All I could do was wait and hope. I tried to calm my racing heart, but panic rose in my throat. In a fit of hysteria, I let out a high-pitched scream which caused more spasms. My body convulsed, and I gasped as I struggled to breathe. My vision blurred, and darkness came once more.

The sound of chanting and an explosion of energy jolted me back to reality. A circle of ancestors surrounded me, smearing my blood across their foreheads. Their chanting grew louder as they danced in some ritual. My voice was all I had to stop them. "Would you betray the child you created? As I lie here dying, you would use my blood to gain immortality?" I yelled at them. "I would rather be in pain than spend my final hours with those who betrayed me."

Their shadows dissipated into thin air, leaving me alone in the cave. I grew ice cold and the sound of my teeth chattering filled my ears. Again, tears spilled from my eyes, but this time it was sadness. I was overwhelmed, alone, and trapped in this cave with no way out. I closed my eyes and prayed for someone or something to rescue me. I waited for what seemed like an eternity, but nothing happened. I had to face the truth that I would probably die.

As I glanced around the cave, I realized I had things to be grateful for. I had the affection of my adoptive parents and the joy I experienced with them. I had met my biological parents, whom I'd searched for my whole life. I had found a friend in Brandon. Knowing I would never be able to express my gratitude for his kindness and support filled me with deep sadness. I had destroyed the Dark Spirits and freed the supernatural world from their terror and was finally able to unleash the full power of my magic. Lastly, I understood why I had always struggled as a witch.

I prayed once more, asking God for one last miracle, and then waited patiently for death to take my life.

****

As my eyelashes fluttered open, the cave came into view. I knew I was still alive. The boulders and rocks that once covered my legs vanished. Strange sounds echoed inside the cave: beeping, humming, buzzing, and distorted voices. Flashes of light blinded me, and I shielded my eyes.

As someone drew my hand away, they said, "Stay still, Raven."

I recognized that voice. My eyes flew open. The cave once again came into view, but I was surrounded by men and women in white lab coats, their faces obscured by hospital masks. I blinked and looked again. A gasp flew out of my mouth as I recognized the eyes of my adoptive parents standing over me. In a state of confusion, I lay there shaking, trying to make sense of what was happening.

A warm hand surrounded mine as a male voice said, "Stay with me, Raven." I looked up into Brandon's hazel eyes staring down at me. He smiled, his dimples deepening as he spoke. "It's going to be okay."

As I gawked at him, I shook my head and asked, "How are you here?"

His hand tightened around mine as he assured, "I've been here the whole time."

My eyes grew wide as fear and confusion took hold. "I'm stuck in the cave. The rocks fell on me. I'm trapped. You have to help me!"

"Raven, stay calm," my adoptive mother said, injecting something into my veins.

As the cave spun around me, I felt warmth spread over my body and I stopped shaking. "Help me," I mumbled. "I'm trapped. Pleas..." My eyelids grew heavy, and I fought to keep them open, but the drug won. I drifted into an abyss of unconsciousness, hoping someone would find me soon.

****

My mother's voice entered my subconscious: "Raven, open your eyes."

As her words filled my head, my eyelids fought to open. Feeling groggy and disoriented, I lifted them halfway. My mother's face blurred in my vision as my eyelids closed. I blinked several times before forcing them wide open, my gaze meeting hers. She sat next to me in the dirt. She brushed her hand down my cheek as she said, "There's those beautiful brown eyes."

My voice trembled as I tried to speak. I shook my head and looked away.

"You're safe," she said, holding my hand tightly. "I won't let anything happen to you."

"Then help me! I'm trapped in this cave."

"You're in the hospital, Raven, not the cave. You've been here for three weeks," she said as she stroked my head and tucked a strand of hair behind my ear.

A sigh escaped my lips as I glanced around me, watching the darkness of the cave meet my gaze. I turned away from her and tried to process her words. As the reality of the situation set in, I felt a weight on my chest. I did not believe her. "No, no, no. I'm in the cave. I'm lying in the dirt."

"You must be blocking everything out as it was too painful. Was accepting the cave and death safer for you?"

I furrowed my brows, not understanding what she was saying. I started to feel claustrophobic. I was desperate for the truth. I needed to do something to ease this paranoia.

She put her fingertips on each side of my head and softly said, "I will help you break down the imaginary walls your mind has built and bring you into the present and this hospital room if you are truly ready."

I closed my eyes and focused on my breathing, letting her guide me. "Yes, I'm ready."

"Repeat after me. Phantom reflections, break apart."

As I opened my eyes to stare into hers, I mimicked her words. "Phantom reflections, break apart."

"One by one, imaginary walls I command you to fall."

"One by one, imaginary walls I command you to fall."

"Look at the world with your eyes and trust your heart."

"Look at the world with your eyes and trust your heart."

Spears of light punctured through the cave and color flashed before my eyes. Green walls, a chrome railing surrounding a hospital bed, and blue blankets filled my vision. Fluorescent lights drew my attention to a figure lying motionless in the bed. A machine to the right of the bed, beeping steadily, was the only sound in the room.

My gaze centered on the figure. As the person came into focus, I realized it was me. Casts enclosed both my legs which were suspended by a cable attached to the ceiling. Sweat laced my pale forehead, and my body trembled every so often. My mother sat next to me in a chair, dressed in an angora sweater and faded jeans. She held tightly to my hand.

The machine beeped again, and reality crashed on top of me, leaving me broken and scared. A dull pain traveled swiftly down my back and into my legs, growing sharper and sharper. Nausea turned my stomach as the room spun about me. I closed my eyes and tried to keep my balance, but the floor seemed to shift and sway beneath me. I wrapped my arms around my body in an attempt to hold myself together while tears flowed down my cheeks. As I gazed into the hospital room, the cave vanished from my vision.

I felt the strength in my mother's voice as she said, "It's going to be okay."

"I don't understand. Why would I choose to stay in that horrible place?"

"It's important to remember that sometimes it's not about what we can comprehend but about what we can't. The power of our own minds can play tricks on us."

I swallowed hard as my frown cut deeper into my forehead. Tricks? Was that what happened in the cave? What could have been so terrible that I chose to stay there? I looked up at my mother and asked, "How did I get out? What happened?"

Her gaze remained fixed on me for a brief moment, perhaps considering whether or not to tell me. She finally spoke, her voice trembling slightly. "The cave collapsed on top of you just inside the opening. We rescued you from the cave."

"Why don't I remember?"

"Sometimes the truth can be too much to handle." She took a deep breath and shuddered. "It was a difficult and devastating thing for us all to witness."

My throat tightened as I asked, "Was I crushed?"

"We think you must have performed a spell, since many of the rocks hovered high above you." Her voice was just above a whisper as she replied, "Several areas of your body were completely covered with rocks." She glanced at my legs. "Mostly your legs. Osiris and I kept you alive by feeding you our blood, but we couldn't heal all your injuries without turning you into a vampire. To truly save you, we brought you here, to the hospital."

"I don't remember any of that." I glanced at the plaster surrounding my legs and heaved a sigh. "Will I be able to walk again?"

Encouragement brightened her eyes as she nodded. "Your adoptive parents say you will but you will have a long road of physical therapy ahead of you."

A wave of emotion washed over me when it dawned on me that my adoptive parents and biological parents had met. What had been said? How did Isis and Osiris introduce themselves? I'm sure my adoptive parents must have freaked from my injuries, not to mention I'd taken off with Brandon only to return damaged and near death, with my biological parents. "Do they know who you are?"

"They do. We made our introductions immediately, making it clear who we were. We wanted a say in the decision regarding your medical treatment to make sure you had the best possible chance of walking again. The four of us were united in our decision regarding your health. They were cooperative and welcoming as if they knew this day would come. It seemed to bother them more that your birthmarks were gone."

My gaze shifted to my arms. "How did you explain that to them?"

"We didn't. They rationalized it as a medical condition."

"I'm not sure how they are going to handle all of this. Though, they never kept anything from me about being adopted. They were always open about that, and about if I ever decided I wanted to search for my biological parents. I will always be grateful for their love and support, but what I was missing from them was the connection to the supernatural world. I had no one to guide me."

She squeezed my hand. "Now, you have your father and I."

As if summoned, my father appeared in the doorway. Relief filled his eyes as he gazed at me.

My mother glanced at him as she said, "She's doing much better."

A weak smile appeared on his face as he bent down to hug me.

"I'm sorry," I said. "You were right. I wasn't prepared. The task overwhelmed me."

"All I care about is that you are safe now." He kissed the top of my head and then turned to my mother. "I was able to connect with Nico. We can stay with him at his place. It's almost sunrise, Isis. We should get going."

A knock caught our attention. Brandon stood in the doorway, his gaze on my parents. "May I come in?"

As my father beckoned him into the room, he said, "We were just getting ready to leave. While we are away, can you keep Raven company?"

"Of course."

My father turned to me and said, "We will be staying with Nico. He lives a few streets over, 3365 Mountain View Lane. If you need us, send us a message by thought and we will come immediately."

Before leaving, my mother kissed my cheek.

Brandon snatched the chair my mother was sitting in and asked, "Are you okay?" His concern was evident in his voice.

"I feel much better now," I replied, grateful to see him again.

"I'm glad to hear you're feeling better." He hesitated a moment before continuing, "I can't imagine what you've been through."

Tears welled in my eyes as I nodded.

"It's okay," he said, gently squeezing my hand.

"After the cave collapsed, what exactly happened? I don't remember." I shuddered. "I only remember waking up in the cave. My mother told me some details, but I think she left out others."

"Really? It's like you put yourself in the cave to escape it all. Not sure if telling you is the right thing."

His words caught my attention. Would I be able to handle what had happened or would I retreat back into the cave? I knew I had to face my problems head-on. If I avoided what happened, I would always have questions and never move forward. I had to take the chance. I nodded firmly as I said, "Yes. I want to know."

Chapter 13

"You were running toward us when the cave collapsed. It happened so fast. One minute you were there, the next you were trapped beneath the weight of rocks and dirt. Isis, Osiris, the Council, Caleb, and Margarete shoveled through the debris faster than my human eyes could comprehend. We were all in shock, and completely frantic that we wouldn't get to you in time."

As he spoke, I remembered the haunting rumble of the cave collapsing as if it were happening all over again. Before the rubble fell over me, the earth had quaked with such a deafening roar. The spell I cast deflected rocks from my upper body, sparing me from more devastating effects. Yet, hearing Brandon recount it was no less frightening.

"It wasn't long before they reached you and found you bleeding and unconscious. Half of you was unharmed from the rocks and dirt, and only your legs were affected by the collapse. Everyone was shouting and chaos erupted. Athaliah took charge and instructed Isis and Osiris to mix their blood and give it to you simultaneously before gently pulling you free. Your legs remained damaged even after the bleeding stopped. I remembered that your adoptive parents worked at the hospital. I shouted over everyone that we needed to get to the hospital where they worked. Osiris and Isis agreed."

"What about the ancestors?"

"What about them?"

"They were in the cave with me, trying to use my blood to transform themselves. I told them I would rather die than give them my blood."

"No, that's not true. They were outside with us, and you weren't in the cave either. You were pulled from the wreckage in minutes."

My gaze focused on him. They painted my blood on their faces and danced about, chanting. I was certain I had seen the whole thing in the cave, but was it a hallucination? Perhaps from pain? "I clearly saw them."

"Raven, they left. They seemed to think their presence was making your situation worse."

"They left?"

"Yes. Shortly after we freed you."

I held my head in my hands. How was it that I remembered something so different? Was my mind playing tricks on me? Again, Brandon squeezed my hand, shifting my attention to him. "Was I unconscious the entire time? It all feels like a dream now."

"Yes, and you laid there completely still. You were breathing and your heart was beating steadily, but you didn't respond to stimulation. Everyone was on edge. We had to get to the hospital as soon as possible. The slightest delay could have serious consequences.

"As Osiris and Isis carried you along the pathway, something extraordinary happened. Thousands of twinkling stars and a golden moon illuminated the forest. The moon's rays impaled the shadow people, and they exploded like in a video game. What happened next blew my mind." He leaned forward in his chair and raised his voice. "The trees literally bowed down to you."

"What?"

"Yeah, trees that bow. Unbelievable! The Guardian said the trees did it to honor your sacrifice."

My mouth hung open. I didn't even know what to say to that. As a result of destroying the Dark Spirits and the cave, I must have cleansed the forest and lifted the curse Luna placed on it. The pain I'd suffered was worth it to save the forest and bring it back to its original beauty.

The power of my magic struck me as I glanced at my legs. Surely, it could heal them. My mind then went to the ancestors. Were they the missing pieces of the puzzle? Were they not like my parents as well? My existence wouldn't have been possible without them. Perhaps I was supposed to grant them immortality. A sudden realization came over me. The bridge connecting past and future was me. I had the power to make the ancestors immortal. It became clear to me that I was the one with the ability to grant their request. As their chosen one, my duty was to ensure their legacy lived on forever. The decision was in my hands.

"What is it, Raven?"

His voice shattered my thoughts, and I stared at him for a moment before answering. "I need to summon the ancestors."

It was his turn to stare at me as he seemed unable to process what I'd just revealed. He blinked and then his eyes grew wide. "You're planning to bring them back to life and grant them immortality, aren't you?"

"Yes," I said, my voice thick with conviction.

"Are you sure you want to do this?"

As I considered his question, I tilted my head to one side. I didn't know much about the ancestors. However, their lineage was part of me. I was born into their world as a witch, a link between the past and the future in a chain of magic. In spite of what might happen when I returned them to their human forms and gave them immortality, I had to accept my role and come to terms with their history and mine. "It's a task I must complete. It's important to me that you believe in and trust me."

He held out his hand, waiting for me to take it. "I absolutely believe in you, Raven."

"Thank you, Brandon." I closed my hand around his and felt the warmth and strength of his grip. "As I summon them, you'll be my anchor."

With a nod, he sat upright. "Yes, of course. Whatever you need."

Strength flowed through me as I closed my eyes and recited, "Blood to blood, I summon thee. My ancestors come to me."

I opened my eyes to a haunting, ancient presence shifting through the air as the spirits of three women and four men stood in front of us. They held their heads high, and their eyes glinted with wisdom under their dark cloaks. The same male who consistently spoke did so again. "Please accept our best wishes for a quick recovery, Raven. We are here to help you whenever needed."

"I'd like to clarify a few things."

"Of course."

Holding Brandon's hand tight, I gazed at the ancestors and asked, "After the collapse, I saw you painting my blood on your faces. Why?"

"Our purpose was not to transform ourselves. You were born into our lineage, our creation. Although we are no longer walking this earth, we are your family, and our ritual was intended to heal you."

Shame burned beneath my skin as I lowered my gaze, unable to meet their eyes. I had given them no chance to explain their actions. I had condemned them and refused to listen to any explanation. Instead of being kind and forgiving, I had allowed my anger to dictate my actions. "I am sorry. I didn't realize," I said in a small voice. "I will do whatever is necessary to grant you immortality and return you to your human form."

"Taking responsibility for our actions and inactions is our responsibility, and together we can move forward." The ancestor handed me a bronze needle and a glass bottle filled halfway with glowing liquid. "In order to gain eternal life and return to our human form, you must prick your finger with this needle and squeeze three drops of blood into this bottle. You must also spit into the bottle once and mix the contents before giving it to me. As each of us drinks from the bottle, place the finger from which you bled against our hearts and say: Life begins with blood and bone. Death's bonds are broken. Eternal life begins."

"Yes, I can do that." I pressed the needle against my middle finger and squeezed out three drops of blood into the bottle. I hesitated before spitting into the bottle. What a strange and gross thing to do, but I did it anyway. My emotions soared as I returned the bottle to the ancestors, knowing that everything was about to change forever. My decision weighed heavily on me, but I was optimistic about the possibilities ahead. At that moment, I knew there was no turning back.

Holding my finger against his chest, I recited the words given to me as he drank from the bottle. I repeated the process until everyone had drunk.

Their shimmering hologram-like forms shifted under the fluorescent lights. Their features became clearer, their eyes brighter, and their bodies gradually solidified into living beings. In celebration of their rebirth, they embraced each other, fully restored to their physical forms.

At that moment, my adoptive mother walked into my hospital room. The hooded ancestors that surrounded my bed caused her to stumble. She quickly regained her composure, but confusion formed on her brow. "What is going on here? Who are these people?"

When I was a child, objects floating in the air around me or toys flying off the shelf were explained away as flukes. As I got older, my abilities evolved and I could consciously control objects with my mind. I could make plants grow or move, create small gusts of wind, and even levitate small objects. I spent countless hours practicing my abilities. My adoptive parents tried to convince me that it was just my imagination, but I knew better. It was in my bones, in my blood. While I knew I had magical abilities, I kept them to myself for fear they would not accept them. This was my chance to prove it. In anticipation of another denial, I said, "I'm a witch, and these are my ancestors."

Her eyes widened as she stared at me in disbelief. She tried to speak, but no words came out. Finally, she stammered, "What?"

"I'm a witch," I repeated. "You always looked the other way, but you know it's true. I need you to finally accept me for who I am."

After a few moments, she asked, "What on earth are you talking about?"

"The things that happened to me as a child were my magic, remember? I can control the elements. That is my gift."

It was evident from her furrowed brows and pinched lips, she didn't believe me, just like when I was a child. I sighed, "I'm telling the truth. I have magical powers."

"I've personally witnessed it," Brandon said, defending me.

"If I may," the male ancestor said in his voice calm. "Raven is one of us. Take heed to her words."

"This is ridiculous. I'm going to get your father." She hurried out of the room without waiting for a reply.

After a moment of trying to comprehend what had just happened, I knew I was heading toward a confrontation with my adoptive parents. I felt like I was a child again, and they were arguing that my powers were all in my imagination. However, I wasn't a child anymore. I was an adult, and once again, I was telling the truth. They needed to listen to me, or I would have to convince them otherwise. I blew out an exasperated breath. "Was I wrong to blurt it out like that?"

"You weren't wrong," Brandon softly said, keeping his gaze on the ancestors. "The hooded cloaks you all have on didn't help. Wearing something that conceals your identity makes people suspicious."

The ancestor examined his attire before asking, "What's wrong with what I'm wearing?"

Brandon stood up and pointed to himself. "We don't dress like that. T-shirts and jeans are the norm. At least take your hoods off," he said, with a brushing motion over his head. "That might help you look less conspicuous."

The ancestors exchanged glances and slowly took off their hoods. Their long flowing hair cascaded past their shoulders. A sense of power emanated from their eyes as they stood side-by-side.

Brandon nodded his approval. "That's better."

Their clothes were the least of my concerns. If my dad wasn't in surgery, he and my mom would rush back to my hospital room and panic. They'd say I was just experiencing delusions or making things up. My friends would be told to leave, claiming they were a bad influence on me and endangering my health.

"You are superior to them," the male ancestor said as he approached my bedside. "Why are you so upset about this?"

"I am not trying to be superior to anyone. I'm just afraid they won't accept the truth and cause a scene."

"You have the power of persuasion. You will convince them."

My parents appeared before I could respond, bringing four security guards with them. As the armed guards stood by the door, their hands resting on their weapons, they kept a vigilant eye on Brandon and the ancestors.

"Visiting hours have ended, and you must leave," one of them said firmly.

Neither Brandon nor the ancestors attempted to move.

Another security guard gestured toward the door and ordered, "You have one minute to leave."

In response, Brandon and the ancestors reluctantly approached the door, but their gaze remained fixed on me. I was unable to move because of my legs, so I used my only weapon, my voice. "You brought security! That wasn't necessary. All you had to do was believe me." I jerked my head toward Brandon and the ancestors. "Don't leave."

My dad leveled his gaze at me before shifting it to the guards. "See them out," he said.

A rigid wave of my hand slammed the door shut. "No! No!" I shouted. My power magnified, causing the fluorescent lights to flicker and the bed to quake. Every second, my power grew stronger, surging through my veins. As my eyes focused on my legs, an intense fever arose inside of me. The room erupted in white light as I whispered, "Connect my bones and restore their strength. Free me of these constraints."

Brandon hurried to me, his eyes wide as he squeezed my hand and said, "I've got you."

As the ceiling cables snapped, the casts surrounding my legs shattered, sending plaster flying across the room. I closed my eyes and imagined my body becom-ing whole again. My muscles flexed with renewed strength as my bones reunified. With the grace of a cat, I leapt to my feet and con-fronted my parents. "Are you now convinced of my claims? Here is the proof you need," I declared.

Awed by my spell, the ancestors nodded in approval. My parents exchanged horrified glances, blood draining from their faces. They grabbed onto each other to keep themselves from collapsing. Wide-eyed, the guards gazed at me before regaining their composure and attempting to restrain me.

"Let her go," my dad said. His voice cracked slightly, betraying the deep pain he tried to conceal.

With sadness in their eyes, my adoptive parents stepped aside and let us go. The ancestors opened the door and motioned for me to follow. As I took Brandon's hand and walked toward the doorway, my parents stared at the ground. While walking out the door, I glanced back at them. Seeing their eyes filled with tears broke my heart, and guilt consumed me.

Chapter 14

While the ancestors headed to Nico's to update my mother and father, Brandon and I headed to my adoptive parents' house. The smell of lavender greeted me when I opened the door. Brandon and I walked into the house, and I shuddered with sadness. I gazed at the pictures and artwork on the walls that chronicled years of treasured memories. My mother's voice filled my head as she said, "Pack a small bag of your belongings and come to Nico's. We can't wait to see you."

A mix of textures, colors, and furniture set the vibe for my bohemian bedroom. My bed was adorned with tons of pillows, and a beige tapestry hung above the reclaimed wooden headboard. Both my closet and dresser were stocked with my favorite clothes. As Brandon grabbed two duffle bags from my closet's top shelf and placed them at the foot of my bed, I quickly changed into a T-shirt and jeans in the bathroom, shedding the hospital gown.

As I glanced around my room, the realization of my circumstances hit. Nostalgia and wretchedness filled me. It had been a place I called my own, filled with memories and items that held a special place in my heart. However, now, my home was a stranger to me. The security and solitude of this room had lost its purpose. The man and the woman who had raised me for 19 years were also strangers. My journals tucked away inside the chest at the end of my bed would be forgotten. A new world, full of discoveries, would replace the bubble-like world I had lived in.

As my heart ached, my eyes welled up with tears, and I did nothing to stop them. They flowed down my cheeks and dotted my duffle bags. Brandon embraced me as he whispered, "Everything will be fine."

As he held me, tears welled up in my eyes. The weight on my shoulders felt lighter, as if he, too, carried some of the burden. It didn't matter how difficult things got, I knew he was there for me. He comforted and protected me like a warm blanket. His presence filled me with a sense of stability I had never felt before. He was my rock, my friend, my confidant. He was my person.

I gathered some jeans, shirts, shoes, underwear, toiletries, and some makeup. Once I had filled both bags, I zipped them shut and released a deep sigh. "I guess I'm ready."

He pulled out his phone and tapped the screen. A moment later, he looked at me. "Uber will be here in five minutes." He swung both bags over his shoulder. "Would you like me to come with you to Nico's?"

l felt safer having him by my side. I grabbed his hands tightly, seeking comfort in his presence. "Yes, please."

His adorable dimples appeared as he smiled sweetly. "Okay."

I looked around my room, gazing at the memories attached to its walls. They whispered goodbye, reminding me of the laughter and tears that shaped me into the person I was today. A touch of nostalgia filled the air as I walked away, leaving me longing for the familiar. With a last glance, I closed the door behind me and walked out of my childhood home.

As I stood on the porch next to Brandon, I breathed in the fresh air. While it was bittersweet to leave the place I had called home for so long, I was also excited to begin the next chapter of my life.

****

It took us about 15 minutes to get to Nico's. Daylight was in full force, so we entered Nico's house carefully to avoid any beams of sunlight following us inside. My mother and father were waiting for us in the sleek, modern living room dominated by black-and-white furniture. As soon as their eyes caught sight of me, my parents rushed toward me. My mother's embrace was particularly long. "I'm so glad you're here, my child." She whispered in my ear.

"I'm glad I'm here with you, too."

We stayed in each other's arms for a few moments before Nico's voice pulled us apart. "Heading back to bed. Let me know if you need anything."

"Thank you, Nico," my mother replied before turning to me and gesturing to the sofa. "Come, sit."

The three of us sat on the sofa together, and Brandon sat in a chair next to us.

"I know you must find all of this difficult," my mother said in a calming voice. "But our work is far from over. You are at the beginning of your magical journey. Preparation must be made. Your debutante ball must be planned. Announcements need to be sent out. On that night you will officially enter the supernatural society."

As her words sank in, I uttered, "What?"

My mother laughed as she said, "It's tradition. You are our daughter, a supreme being who will rule over supernatural creatures. We must introduce you to our world."

My head spun as I stared at her. Her words felt like a distant dream, but I knew they were true: I was a goddess's daughter.

"The ball is extravagant, dressed to the nines in tuxedos and gowns. Champagne will flow, and you'll dance and mingle with hundreds of guests." My father winked at me, his eyes twinkling with delight. "And there might even be a challenge or two. It will be an unforgettable night."

I blinked several times as I asked, "Challenges? Why?"

In a matter-of-fact tone, he responded. "Some may test your abilities and magic. You must be prepared to show them what you are capable of. Be confident and persuasive so they never doubt your valor."

"You will also need a protector," my mother added, "as there may be others who covet your talents. Always be aware of your surroundings. Consider your actions and trust your intuition. A good protector will guard you from those who would exploit your talents. Moreover, you must trust and rely on your protector, and he or she needs to be willing to fight if necessary. The ancestors are of the highest court of witches. They will be your council and can help you with this decision."

A flutter of nerves swelled in my stomach. I took a deep breath, trying to remain calm. I glanced over at Brandon. A bewildered expression tugged at his brows. He seemed just as confused and anxious as I was. Suddenly, he rose from his seat and said, "Hey, Raven, I need to leave. My parents keep blowing up my phone." After nodding at my parents, he headed for the door.

My heart ached as I watched him walk away. A thought crossed my mind: *give him your number*. "Brandon, wait."

His gaze shifted to mine as he turned.

As I held up my cell phone, I said, "We never exchanged numbers."

"Add your number," he said as he handed me his phone. I typed it in and returned his phone to him.

"Texting you," he said.

As he walked out the door, my phone chimed. A smile spread across my face as I read his text, *Will call you soon.* Then it dawned on me. Staying at Nico's was only a temporary fix due to the sun. Where would my parents take me? To their home? Where was that? I had no idea. With a sigh, I turned and faced them. "So, what happens next? I'm assuming we aren't staying with Nico."

My mother softly laughed. "Your assumptions are correct. Our home is in Scotland at the Council's Haven. Your brother, Horus, and your aunt, Nephthys, live in a beautiful seaside villa in Italy."

A new country was not on my agenda. The idea of adjusting to a completely different environment thousands of miles away made my stomach churn. Seattle was my place in the world. Plus, Brandon was here. I never had a friend before, especially one who I'd had a strong connection with. I couldn't leave him behind, and I didn't want to lose his friendship either. "I could get my own place here in Seattle."

They exchanged glances before they turned their gazes on me. My father hesitated for a moment before he said, "We think it's best if you stay with us for now. Living alone would make you vulnerable to harm. Our resources will ensure your safety."

I couldn't stay with them forever. I had to make my own way in the world. "But I need to prove I'm capable of protecting myself. I'd rather take the risk than hide under your roof."

"Things are different now," my mother explained. "The supernatural world will sense your presence. Others will seek you out. You must stay close to us. We'll watch over you."

"I can recruit the protector that you talked about. I will ask Jaffa. I trust her and I am confident she will understand how important it is for me to remain independent."

My father shook his head. "It's not about independence. It's about preventing threats before they happen."

"Jaffa is an experienced fighter," I argued. "She knows what to look out for and how to handle any possible danger."

"The only way to ensure your safety is to anticipate threats before they happen," he said, continuing to drive his point.

The decision was not up for debate. I was an adult, not a child. I could live wherever I wanted. I realized we had just become a family. I wasn't saying I would never see them, but moving across the globe was not going to happen. I was very clear about my intentions, and they wouldn't change my mind. I needed to stand up for myself and make the decision that was best for me. "I'm 19. I don't need your permission to get my own place."

As my father rose from the sofa, he towered over me. "It doesn't matter how old you are," he said harshly, his eyes narrowing. "You are the daughter of gods, a magical being. Life will never be the same as it once was."

He made me feel like a child being scolded. Having destroyed the threat against me, I had no interest in being paranoid or imagining what might happen. "I am quite capable of protecting myself. I don't need a babysitter."

My mother leapt between us before my father responded to my sarcasm. As she placed her hand on his shoulder, she said, "Please, let's not argue. I think I have come up with a solution. We can buy a house in here." She turned to me. "You can still live in Seattle if you live with us."

My mother's suggestion surprised me. I hadn't expected her to come up with such a sensible solution. As I nodded, I felt relief that my parents were willing to compromise to ensure that I would be able to remain here, easing my anxiety. "That's fair. Thank you," I replied.

"Now that we've reached an understanding, I think your father and I need some sleep. Perhaps you do, too."

Although it was midday, my body and mind were exhausted. "I could use some rest."

"There are two guest rooms upstairs. Come, let me show you," my father said as he grabbed my duffle bags.

My parents led me up the stairs and into a room directly across the hall from theirs. They kissed me on the cheek before leaving me on my own. The rose-colored bedroom certainly wasn't Nico's style. In contrast to the black and white theme of his first floor, the girly, dainty bedroom gave me warm fuzzy feelings and reminded me of my old room.

I laid my cell phone on the nightstand before curling up with a pillow on the queen-size bed. With a deep breath, I rested my hand over my heart, filled with contentment. My journey was just beginning. From a young age, I dreamed of finding my parents, learning about my past, and discovering the power that ruled my body. But what would happen next?

In the midst of my joy, nervousness overcame me as the ball entered my mind. There would be hundreds of guests, dancing, and challenges. As I trembled, I gripped the pillow even tighter. I had so many questions. What would I wear? How would I behave? Most importantly, who would attend? The supernatural world would view me from a pedestal at the ball. It wasn't like I was a socialite. Was my role to act the part? But I was an outsider. I had been alone and considered a freak most of my life. I shook the negative thoughts away and reminded myself that my destiny was in my hands.

My cell phone rang, interrupting my insecurities. I glanced at the number and smiled. "Hi, Brandon."

"Hi Raven, sorry I left so suddenly. To tell the truth, your parents' explanation about the ball, how you need a protector, and all that other stuff freaked me out a bit. I hope I didn't make it awkward for you."

"No, it's okay. I feel the same way. All of this is weird for me, too. Sorry, my parents went overboard on the whole ball thing, but you'll come, right?

"Yes, of course. I'm looking forward to it." He replied. He hesitated for a moment. "I hope I'm on the guest list." He laughed. "I don't want to be that guy who crashes the party."

After mulling over his words, I wondered, *What prompted him to believe he was not on the guest list? Was he under the impression that the ball was only for close family and friends? He was the only person I wanted there. Didn't he realize that?* "Of course, you're invited." I made a mental note to make sure my mother sent him an invitation.

"Then I wouldn't miss it for the world."

A flush of warmth radiated from my cheeks, and my heart raced with excitement. I was relieved and delighted that he would be spending the evening with me.

Chapter 15

The day finally arrived after weeks of preparation. My bedroom at the Council's Haven buzzed with energy as makeup artists, hair stylists, and event coordinators prepared me and my mother for the ball. The makeup artists applied foundation, blush, and eyeshadow to achieve a flawless look, while the hair stylists crafted intricate braids and curls. Throughout the process, the event coordinators ensured that every detail was perfect and that my mother and I were ready on time.

I was in awe of how beautiful my mother looked with her long hair braided with gems and dressed in an off-the-shoulder royal blue gown. The event coordinators picked out sparkling diamond earrings and a necklace to complete my mother's elegant look. The clock ticked closer to the start of the ball, creating an atmosphere of anticipation.

"Raven, you look absolutely breathtaking in that lace dress," she said, taking my hands in hers.

Seeing myself in the mirror, I felt as if I were a living doll with my hair cascading past my shoulders, my eyes framed by gorgeous, thick lashes, and my lips accentuated by pink lipstick. I twirled in a circle, eyeing the hand-beaded lace trumpet gown with a V-neckline that hugged every curve. The intricate beads shimmered in the light, giving the dress a glamorous and romantic touch. I blushed as my hands swept over my cheeks.

An expression of joy played across her red lips as she tightly embraced me. Holding me at arm's length, she said, "I am so excited to accompany you to your event. Are you ready?"

My heart raced as I fidgeted with my dress. *Was I ready?* Probably not, but I was the guest of honor. I knew this was supposed to be my moment to shine, but doubt and uncertainty gnawed at me, questioning whether I was truly prepared for this momentous occasion. However, there was also a sense of curiosity and determination to prove to myself that I could conquer any challenges that came my way too. There was no turning back now. "I'm ready," I answered with a confident tone.

My mother gently guided me out of the room and into the hallway where my father was waiting. His stylish black tuxedo and bow tie complemented his dapper appearance. His lips parted into a charming smile as his gaze centered on my mother. He kissed her cheek and said softly, "You always take my breath away." He caught sight of me, and his eyes widened. He hugged me as he said, "You're a vision of loveliness, Raven. This is the beginning of your new journey and I am honored to introduce you to our world."

My parents held my hands as we descended the spiral staircase. Beneath the ornate ceiling, the polished marble floor glistened with the bright colors of the gleaming chandeliers. The ancestors, my brother, my aunt, and Brandon were waiting for us in the circular foyer.

Upon descending the spiral staircase, I thought, *Here we go.* My father's firm grip assured me of his support, while my mother's warm smile confirmed her love. Throughout the sparse foyer, elegance ruled. A vase of freshly arranged lilies dominated the narrow console table, releasing a delightful scent. Plants adorned the walls and ceilings, bringing the outside world into the space and creating a serene and calming ambiance.

The ancestors looked magnificent in their tailored dark tux-edos and sparkling gowns. Jewels adorned the women's hair, while a ponytail neatly tied back the men's. My aunt wore a gor-geous red gown that was sophisticated and form-fitting. She wore her hair twisted into a bun, with loose curls framing her face. A simple pearl necklace completed her classic look. Horus looked sharp in a black tuxedo and crisp white linen shirt. A black and white striped bow tie complemented his clean-shaven face. With his charisma and confidence, the vampire god looked prepared for any situation.

Despite all their amazing looks, Brandon's modern style cap-tured my attention with his slim-fitting black tuxedo and burgun-dy bow tie. He had his hair slicked back, tucked behind his ears, and his hazel eyes sparkled with excitement as he glanced at me. It made my pulse race just thinking about dancing with him.

With my parents by my side, I entered the grand foyer. As I walked beneath the stunning chandeliers above, the sound of my heels clicking on the polished marble floor echoed in the silence. I couldn't shake the feeling that I might not meet their expecta-tions. What if I stumbled or misspoke in front of everyone? To make them proud, I would do everything in my power to prevail.

"Your guests won't be able to take their eyes off of you," my aunt said, kissing my cheek.

Returning her kiss, I said, "Thank you."

As Horus bobbed his chin at me, he advised, "Keep focused, be on your guard, and never turn down a challenge."

While I narrowed my gaze and conveyed understanding, the butterflies in my stomach said otherwise. Although I knew I was capable, I had no idea what challenges would be ahead. Again, I doubted my strength and ability, but I would keep that a secret from everyone.

The ancestors' presence exuded support and calmness as they gathered around me, their ancient faces adorned with wisdom and understanding. They seemed to be able to tap into my emotions and read my mind. As their positive energy emanated from them, they soothed my fears and instilled a newfound sense of security in me, alleviating my doubts. One of the women said, "Believe in yourself, and nothing is impossible."

As I stood there, looking at the line of ancestors, a realization dawned on me—I didn't have a clue what their names were. All these people who had shaped my life and my history, and I didn't even know their names. It made me feel a sense of responsibility and desire to connect with them on another level. "Would you please introduce yourselves to me?"

The same male, who was clearly in charge of the group, spoke first. "I am Leif, a spirit conjurer. I can control movements and actions, bind spirits to specific people and places, and prevent them from harming anyone." He then moved down the row of ancestors and began introductions, starting with the females. "This is Farina."

"I possess the power of shadow conjuring and can summon and manipulate shadows as I wish," Farina said. "It is a pleasure to meet you."

"It's nice to meet you, too."

"This is Tarja."

Tarja greeted me with a slight smile. "Hello, Raven. I am an air sorceress and can use my magic to create storms, tornadoes, and other powerful natural phenomena."

"Hello, Tarja."

"This is Smara."

"I am an energy bender," Smara said. "I have the power to create illusions, bend reality, and summon creatures and objects. I'm looking forward to getting to know you."

"I am as well."

Leif approached the first male and said, "This is Aidan."

Aidan reached for my hand as he said, "It's very nice to meet you. I am a teleporter, capable of teleporting myself anywhere in the blink of an eye. I am also able to transport objects and people."

"Nice to meet you, too."

"This is Frewin."

With serious eyes, Frewin nodded at me. "I am a clairvoyant. I see the future, as well as read minds. I can also project my thoughts onto others."

I returned the nod, though my expression was less intense.

"Last but not least, this is Zander."

"Hello," Zander said. "I am a soul bender with the ability to manipulate souls for my own benefit. I use my powers to control souls to make them loyal to me. I can also use my magic to heal others."

After acknowledging Zander, I addressed the ancestors. "As my council, I will need your wisdom, experience, and guidance in navigating this supernatural world. While I assure you I will do my best, I am completely unfamiliar with any of this."

Leif gestured to himself and the rest of the ancestors as he said, "The gift of immortality you have given us will never be forgotten. You have our support, and we are committed to protecting you and the supernatural world."

My mother interrupted as she directed everyone toward a stone archway and into a dimly lit corridor. "Let's not keep our guests waiting."

My heart pounded in my ears, matching the frantic rhythm of my breathing. Fear and determination drove me forward, as I swore to face whatever lay ahead.

Brandon caught up to me and whispered in my ear, "You look absolutely beautiful."

I giggled and nudged his shoulder as I whispered back, "Thank you, and you look very handsome."

His dimples appeared as he returned the nudge. "Thank you. My kid sister helped me pick out my tux."

I confirmed, "She did well."

Our footsteps echoed in the empty hallway as we headed to the ball. The flickering wall sconces created a magical atmosphere, illuminating the path to my destiny. Although I anticipated an exciting evening, the unknown cast a shadow over the ball. I forced myself to embrace the possibilities of the ball despite my fears.

My parents approached two large wooden doors. Ornate brass handles gleamed in the soft light, enhancing their dark, rich color. As the doors opened, lush floral arrangements and embellished ceiling moldings filled the lavish ballroom. Standing in the doorway, I gazed up at the majestic crystal chandeliers illuminating the room. The hum of conversation, the gentle clinking of glasses, along with the aroma of roses and lilies, welcomed me into the room. Another chandelier hung above the dance floor, highlighting the intricate wood carvings.

Upon entering, I was transported into a world of enchantment and excitement. The stunning sights around me overwhelmed my mind, making me unsure where I should begin. Throughout the room, elegant tablecloths, trimmed with delicate lace, shimmered softly under the ceiling lights. Centerpieces featured crystal vases filled with vibrant blooms, echoing the floral theme. Tall, gilded mirrors lined the walls and reflected the chandelier's warm light. Handcrafted chairs surrounded every table, and guests wore stunning gowns and handsomely tailored tuxedos. A jeweled neckline and wristlet gave their outfits an air of elegance.

An orchestra of beautifully dressed musicians and dazzling instruments sat across from the dance floor. An enormous table on a raised platform dominated the center of the room nearby. Besides its exquisite woodwork and beautifully crafted edges and legs, the table was flanked by five throne-like chairs.

As my parents led us to that table, I realized that none of the five chairs were meant for Brandon. Brandon's deliberate exclusion from our dinner table sent a wave of disappointment through me. I turned to my parents and asked, "Where is Brandon sitting?"

My father placed his hand on my shoulder and pointed to a table directly to the right of ours. "He will join Rick, Hypatia, Jaffa, Eve, Margarete, and Caleb at their table."

"We have surrounded you by individuals who will have a profound impact on your journey," my mother explained. "Alongside Brandon's table, we have Luna, the ancestors, and the Council to our left, and the Ten at a table adjacent to the Council's."

My gaze met Brandon's as he took my hand in his and softly said, "Those chairs are for your family. It's okay."

Shaking my head, I said, "You should be sitting next to me."

A slight smile touched his lips. "I'll be close to you."

My mother hugged me tight and ensured, "It will only be for a short while. Once introductions have occurred, you may leave the table."

As her words reached my ears, my tension eased away. I leaned into her and whispered, "Thank you."

After stepping onto the platform, I inhaled deeply, letting the butterflies in my stomach flutter wildly. It was time to smile confidently, as the spotlight was on me. Guests stopped their discussions and took their seats. The room buzzed with excitement as they whispered among themselves, keeping their eyes fixed on me. The soft hum of conversations was broken by the gentle scrape of chair legs against the floor as people shifted into their seats.

My father and mother stood before the crowd while Horus, Nephthys, and I sat on gold and platinum thrones. The waiting was torturous for me. I fidgeted with the beads on my dress, trying to ignore the butterflies fluttering in my stomach. Soon I would be announced as the daughter of Isis and Osiris. One wrong move on my part would ruin my chances of proving myself.

My father spread his arms wide as he said, "Welcome. Thank you all for coming. Nineteen years ago Isis and I were blessed with a child." His eyes gleamed with admiration as he looked at me. "My heart is filled with pride and awe for our beautiful daughter. She possesses the intelligence and charisma of gods, the mystical powers of witches, and the compassion and empathy of humans. Reflecting the magnificence of all three worlds, she is indeed a rare and unique tribrid. I can't help but feel blessed to be a part of her extraordinary existence."

My body trembled with excitement and fear as I considered the immense responsibilities of my father's faith in me. On the one hand, I was grateful for his support and belief in my abilities, but on the other hand, the weight of living up to his expectations and the knowledge of the powers I possessed scared the hell out of me. It was both an honor and a terrifying realization to know that I carried the essence of three different entities within me.

"I am delighted to introduce you to our daughter," he said, motioning for me to stand up. "Raven, I give you our world."

Two blonde-haired men surrounded us. Their aggressive body language exuded power and authority, as they pointed at me and loudly proclaimed their disbelief. "We challenge the veracity of this progeny."

As their dark eyes penetrated my soul, I shivered and brushed the chill off my arm. Was this my first challenge?

My father's voice bellowed anger as he drew the tension in the room. "Sobek, Khum, we are members of the Ten, an alliance that has stood strong for centuries. Let us work together, not question each other's words."

My mother, her own frustration evident, shot back, "I can assure you that we speak the truth. To suggest we are lying is an insult."

The Ten's table had two empty chairs, and a third vampire had left his seat. The men confronting my parents were vampire gods. A cold glare settled inside the third vampire's emerald-green eyes as he stepped onto the platform. The soft glow of the chandeliers reflected off his bronzed skin and jet-black hair. He directed that icy stare at my parents as he accused rather than asked, "How does it feel when you are challenged for speaking the truth?"

My mother rolled her eyes and groaned. "Really, Amon? Nineteen years later, you're still grudgeful."

Grudgeful for what, I thought.

With a swagger that exuded confidence, he threw his shoulders back as he replied, "I am." His eyes narrowed. "You robbed Beth and I of five years."

My gaze bounced back and forth between my parents and him. What was he talking about?

My father glared back at the vampire Amon, declaring, "It is I who am now asking you to stand by our side and defend our words."

"The same way you defended mine?"

More vampires vacated the Ten's table, forming a circle around us. Their presence filled the once peaceful surroundings with tension. The unspoken hostility between Amon and my parents was obvious as they stood facing each other. A beautiful redhead rushed to Amon's aid, putting her pale hand on his arm, and saying, "We are guests here. It's not the right time nor place to dredge up the past."

A tall vampire with a neatly trimmed beard and a slim, attractive female vampire with short, jet-black hair joined Amon.

My brother suddenly rose from his and boasted, "I have tasted Raven's blood. Our parents speak the truth."

In unison, our parents spun around and faced him, shock etched into their raised eyebrows and gaped mouths. "You did what?" my father uttered.

"I had to," he claimed. "You both had just been abducted, and this girl shows up claiming to be your daughter. I couldn't just take her at her word."

"I actually informed you, not Raven," Caleb corrected.

Horus waved him away. "Small details." He faced our parents. "As far as I knew, I had no sister. It had to be proven, and blood doesn't lie."

My mother shook her head and held up her hands as she muttered, "Horus, I can't even…I'll deal with you later." She turned her back on him, and he sulked back into his seat.

Adding a curt nod, Sobek said, "I will taste her blood as well."

Khum quickly followed suit, "And I."

As my aunt wrapped her protective arm around me, I clutched my throat.

"You will do no such thing," my father growled.

The ancestors left their table and approached. In typical Leif fashion, he stepped forward and said, "I can explain. Raven was conceived by our magic and DNA from Osiris and Isis. She is their daughter, and this explanation should suffice. There is no need to shed blood."

"It does not suffice," Sobek proclaimed. "Her blood must be consumed."

Khum agreed. "I second it. Therefore, it must be done."

The blood thieves raged on before me in a fierce vampire showdown that escalated into total mayhem. My aunt hid me under the table as she and Horus flew across the table at incredible speed. Their eyes glowed with intensity, and their fangs glistened with saliva. Their heated growls shook me to my core. I squeezed my eyes shut and clapped my hands over my ears, drowning out the sound. Hiding under the table like a frightened mouse, I rocked back and forth, my mind racing with thoughts of survival. Every sound intensified my vulnerability. There had to be a way out.

My skin tingled with magic in that moment, inviting me to unleash its power. Leaving my hiding place, I extended my arms and bowed to the heavens as an otherworldly breeze swept through my hair. My fingertips spun a vortex of magic around the vampires. With three words, "I enslave you," I bound the vampires and rendered them helpless.

After neutralizing the dispute, I released the vampires from my spell with a wave of my hand and sent them back to their seats.

They sat staring at me, confused as to how I could suspend their supernatural power. I stood before them triumphant. I curtsied and sarcastically declared, "I have conquered my first challenge. Regarding my birth, I was born out of power and not love. Because my family did not provide answers, I relied heavily on books for guidance. During my quest to understand who I was as a witch, I experienced numerous trials, had my blood tested, and had my origins and bloodlines challenged. It was with determination and perseverance that I discovered the truth and confirmed my birthright. Please allow me to live my life in peace, complete my journey, and enjoy time with my family."

"You tell them, baby witch," Jaffa shouted from her seat as she pumped her fist into the air.

A smile spread across Brandon's face as he gazed at me and applauded. Immediately, Rick and Hypatia joined in, clapping their hands. Caleb tapped his silverware against his glass before rising to his feet and cheering. Margarete stood next to him, clanking her glass. The remaining guests raised their hands and echoed thunderous applause throughout the room, showing their support for me.

My parents joined my side and embraced me. As my father let go, he put his hands on my shoulders and met my eye level as he said, "No one in this room will ever doubt your abilities again."

"We are so very proud of you," my mother added, squeezing me tightly.

As he turned me toward the Ten's table, my father continued, "These gods will share their wisdom and open your eyes to the hidden realms of the universe. Let me introduce you to them."

After what just happened I thought better of it. The gods seemed unpredictable, and I didn't want a repeat of God vs Magic.

I needed reinforcements. There was only one person I could look to for help—Jaffa.

I stood on my tiptoes to kiss his cheek. "I'll be right back." I dashed off to speak with Jaffa before waiting for a reply.

I stopped a few feet away from her table and waved her over. The chandelier's glow enhanced the radiance of her braids and the sheen of her armor. A smirk came to her lips as she rose from her seat and approached me. She embodied everything I imagined a protector should be. I stood there, my hands fluttering at my sides, hoping she would say yes to my proposal.

Her expression shifted into a more serious demeanor as she addressed me. "What can I do for you, baby witch?"

As I swallowed my nerves back down my throat, I said, "As I reign over this supernatural world, there may be those who plan to harm me. I need a protector to defend me from powerful magical beings, vengeful spirits, and even human vendettas. You have a wealth of experience and skills, and I believe your presence will prove invaluable to me. Would you be willing to serve as my protector?"

She looked at me with a fierce and determined stare that reflected her years of experience as a warrior. With conviction, she said, "I would be honored to be your protector."

As I breathed a sigh of relief, I said, "Thank you so much. And I thought what better time than now to start? My father wants to formally introduce me to the Ten."

A wicked grin curled her charred lips. "I'd love nothing more than to stand by your side and chastise those arrogant vampire gods."

"Let's do it." I led her back to my parents and proudly announced, "Jaffa has agreed to be my protector."

The unwavering loyalty and experience of Jaffa drew my mother's approval, and my father shook her hand as well. "We trust your expertise and reputation," he said. "I know you will make sure that our daughter's safety is your top priority."

With a curt nod, Jaffa replied, "I will protect her at all costs."

"Well, then, let's introduce you to the Ten," my father said, escorting Jaffa and I to their table.

The room was filled with the hum of conversation and the clink of champagne glasses, but my mind was preoccupied with Jaffa's powerful presence. Her every step exuded power and authority, capturing everyone's attention. With her fierce gaze, she left no doubt about her capabilities. I could almost feel the force of her dominance radiating off of her, igniting my own courage. As I stood next to her in front of the Ten, I mimicked the strength and poise of her stance.

As my father wrapped his arm around me, my mother reached for my hand. Their comforting embrace filled me with warmth and reassurance.

"Raven, you already know Hathor," my father said as we faced the goddess.

With a subtle nod, Hathor acknowledged me.

"And next to Hathor, we have Anubis. Anubis, meet Raven."

He rose from his seat and reached for my hand. His maroon-colored lips matched his bow tie, and against his black tuxedo, his pale skin appeared eerie yet captivating. "Your powers seem quite impressive for someone so young. If you ever need help perfecting them, I am happy to assist."

I smiled sweetly and replied, "Thank you. I may take you up on that."

His lips curved into a proud grin.

Hathor sighed and rolled her eyes, clearly unimpressed by Anubis. He waved away her annoyance as he returned to his seat.

In a few steps, we reached the chair where Amon sat. "Raven, this is Amon. Amon, this is Raven."

He stood before me, his long jet-black hair resting on his shoulders. Looking into his emerald-green eyes, my breath quickened as I recalled his words to my parents. As we shook hands, his tall frame conveyed superiority and grace. "It is a pleasure to meet you, Raven," he said.

His handsome face held my attention. "It's nice to meet you, too."

My mother gently nudged me as she pointed to the gorgeous redhead sitting next to him. "This is Beth, Amon's immortal companion."

Her vibrant red hair cascaded down her back in loose waves as she rose to take my hand. Her enchanting eyes resembled the sea and sparkled with kindness. "Hi, Raven. I was naive about this supernatural world once, just like you. If you ever want any pointers, I'm happy to help."

"That's very kind of you. Thank you."

The vampire god sitting in the next chair radiated an aura of power and authority as we continued our introductions. His almond-colored eyes and neatly trimmed beard enhanced his chiseled face. "Ptah, this is Raven," my mother said. "Raven, this is Ptah."

Our hands met and his touch had a kind, unspoken quality that made me feel welcomed. "You are a breath of fresh air to our supernatural world." He placed his hand on the shoulder of the woman sitting next to him and said, "This is my lovely immortal companion, Brit."

Her short black hair was styled in a sleek bob, accentuating her high cheekbones. She smiled at me with her baby-blue eyes and said, "Hello, Raven. Nice to meet you."

"It's nice to meet both of you," I replied, nodding at them.

Reaching the final two chairs, my father stepped forward and folded his arms across his chest, his gaze piercing and unyielding. Behind him, Jaffa stood silently, her tall, athletic frame emitting strength and confidence. As my father spoke, his voice oozed authority. "I am hesitant to introduce these two; however, they are members of the Ten. Therefore, I will. Sobek and Khum, my daughter, Raven."

Neither of them spoke as their dark eyes regarded me, but they did offer a nod. I chose to be the mature one as I said, "Nice to meet you both."

Before Sobek or Khum could respond, my parents whisked me away toward the Council's table. The Council was already familiar to me, so I saw no point in reintroducing myself. I was about to voice my objection when the vampire sitting next to Teresa caught my eye. Dark wavy locks framed his chiseled jawline, and his blue-gray eyes held an irresistible charm that drew me in and held me captive. As he caught me staring at him, his wine-colored lips curved into a seductive smile.

I frowned. Was he flirting with me? He appeared to be Teresa's date, since his arm was wrapped around the back of her chair. Suddenly, his smooth and velvety voice entered my head and said, "Hello, Raven, daughter of Osiris and Isis. I'm Philippe."

Jaffa pulled me aside and whispered in my ear, "He's known for his manipulative ways and isn't to be trusted. Be careful, Raven."

As she spoke, I noticed the vampire's intense gaze still locked on me. I shook off the fascination, laughed, and shooed her away. "Jaffa, I'm not asking him to Netflix and chill. I'm just admiring from afar."

"I haven't the faintest idea what that means."

"It means I'm not interested."

"Ah, perfect. I am your protector after all. Therefore, I must protect."

I rested my hand on her arm and agreed. "Yes, you are, and you have."

My parents stepped back onto the platform, and my father clapped his hands loudly, gaining everyone's attention. "Please join us as we dance the night away to celebrate our daughter's special day." He turned toward the orchestra. "Maestro, let's get the party started!"

The maestro nodded and raised his baton, signaling the musicians. As the lights dimmed, their skilled fingers worked the instruments. The violins soared with a delicate melody, weaving through the air like a gentle breeze. The flutes added a light, airy texture, while the clarinets provided a warm, resonant undertone. As the instruments came to life, guests flocked to the dance floor, captivated by the rich sound.

My parents left me behind to join the other couples on the dance floor. As they waltzed across the floor, they blended seamlessly into the crowd. Jaffa and Kohath, an unlikely couple, were drawn to the dance floor by infectious joy. As I headed back to my seat, Luna stepped into my path. She held open her palms, showing me a crystal pendant necklace. "I have something for you," she said as she gave me the necklace.

The vibrant colors caught the light, sparkling like a kaleidoscope. My mouth dropped as I recognized the array of colors. I was holding my orb. My brows twitched in confusion as I said, "I don't understand."

"The orb told me to give you a message. While it knew the necessity to be near you, its true form was awkward and inconvenient in everyday life. As a result, it became a necklace. Every time you rub the crystal between your palms, the sphere will appear."

The necklace fell softly against my skin as Luna slipped it around my neck and fastened it. As my orb's true form was suspended in the middle of the necklace, I was filled with surprise and gratitude. A sensation of warmth spread through my body as I connected with it again. "I will never take it off. Thank you for sharing my orb's message and gift with me, Luna."

"Of course." Her eyes shifted behind me, and she added, "You have company. Enjoy your party, Raven." She hurried off, leaving me alone with Horus.

He extended his hand and asked, "May I have this dance?"

His face remained expressionless as we took our places on the crowded dance floor. Our hands were interlocked and we glided around the floor on a path of precision and grace. "It was reckless and disrespectful to consume your blood without your consent," he said. "Please accept my apologies for my misguided actions and for any discomfort or harm I may have caused you."

"Mother and Father told you to apologize, didn't they?"

Horus smirked. "But that's not why I did." As we spun in circles, Horus continued, "When I learned about you, I was skeptical. However, after seeing your bravery and selflessness with the Dark

Spirits, I couldn't help but admire and accept you as a sibling. This is why I apologized to you."

As I looked into his eyes, I could see he had spoken the truth. While it wasn't all warm and fuzzy, he saw me for who I really was. I knew we would never be close, but now I had his support and acceptance.

Someone tapped me on the shoulder as the music faded and Horus released my hand. I turned around to find Caleb's hazel eyes twinkling with mischief. He captured my attention with his confident smile and outstretched hand. In a moment of lightheartedness, he offered me a break from Horus. As he bowed before me, he asked, "May I have this dance?"

With a slight curtsy and playful grin, I accepted Caleb's offer. As I stepped into his arms, I prepared myself for Caleb's sarcasm. Taking my hands, he whirled me around the floor, spinning faster and faster. Laughter rose in my throat and spilled out of my mouth. He slowed his pace and took a moment to look me in the eye before saying, "As a rule, I give everyone a nickname, but you were a challenge. It took a while to come up with the appropriate moniker for you. Your courage and strength inspired me to call you, Proud Heart. It's a perfect representation of your personality and spirit. You are one of the few people who can handle my wit and sarcasm. It's my belief that we are on the same level. It's not something I say often, so take it as a compliment."

His words penetrated my heart, giving me a sense of validation and empathy. "I am flattered by the nickname and I love it. Not many vampires can hold a candle to you. You're one in a million. I am grateful to have you as a friend."

"And I yours."

"May I cut in?" My father asked.

"Of course," Caleb replied, releasing me and gesturing for my father to step in.

Caleb nodded. "Raven."

I returned the nod. "Caleb."

As Caleb walked away, my father took my hand. As we danced together, it suddenly became clear to me that love and security surrounded me. It was a reminder that no matter what challenges I faced, he would support me and protect me.

As he gazed down at me, his eyes glowed with affection. "I am so proud to be your father, Raven. You are a miracle to me and your mother. Everything has led up to this moment. I would go through it all over again, just to be here with you now, and call you my daughter. I love you, Raven."

My hand fluttered to my throat as tears of joy moistened my eyes. It was a moment that I will forever cherish and remember, as it solidified our bond. All I could say was, "I love you too, Father."

His warm smile spread across his lips as he hugged me tightly and kissed my forehead. "There's someone who really wants to dance with you but can't quite muster the courage." He bobbed his head toward Brandon's table.

Heat brushed my cheeks as I covered my mouth, giggling. "I've been waiting for him to ask me."

"I think *you* may have to ask him."

I couldn't stop the smile from spreading on my lips as I rushed off to his table. In the process, I passed Margarete and Caleb, as well as Rick and Hypatia, dancing passionately, their gazes locked on each other. Then there was Eve and Luna, partnered with two Council members, twirling them around the dance floor. It was at that moment that I realized that love knows no boundaries and can unite people from all walks of life.

I approached Brandon's table with anticipation. He sat alone, hands clasped, eyes lowered, and his shoe tapping the floor. "Hi, Brandon." I said.

He jerked his head upward. As his eyes fell on me, a warm smile spread across his lips. Rising to his feet, he cleared his throat awkwardly. "Hello, Raven."

I held out my hand. "Come dance with me."

His smile widened. "Okay."

Standing in the middle of the dance floor, he wrapped his arm around my waist and clasped my hand, giving me a sense of love and happiness I had never experienced. As Brandon became my rock, my anchor in the chaos of my past, I couldn't help but think about how lucky I was to have him by my side. I wondered if this was the beginning of an amazing journey together.

He whispered, "I've wanted to dance with you since I saw you walk down the stairs."

"And I with you," I paused, then asked, "Why did you wait?"

He looked at me for a moment, then said, "I don't see myself on the list of your superheroes. Clearly I'm not Superman, and you're well," he looked over at me, "majorly powerful. I didn't think—"

As I cut him off, I smacked his shoulder and said, "Brandon, don't you get it? You *are* my superhero! You took me to Eve, Bloodthirst, Margarete and Caleb, the Council. You helped me discover my past, learn the truth, find my parents. Without you, I wouldn't be the person I am now."

The dimpled smile that I loved so much brightened his face. His eyes searched mine as he asked, "May I kiss you?"

Standing on my tiptoes, I cupped his face in my hands and pressed my lips to his. His arms wrapped around me and he pulled me close. His lips touched mine softly, sending shivers down my spine. As our kiss deepened, the world around us faded away, replaced by a feeling of warmth and belonging. The bustling atmosphere of the room became a distant murmur, replaced by the sound of our racing hearts. At that moment, time seemed to stand still, and a ball of emotions—love, happiness, and a feeling of rightness—enveloped us, leaving no doubt that something extraordinary was about to begin. The need for air pulled us apart.

"I guess that was a yes," he said, grinning.

I laughed softly and nodded. "An absolute yes!"

Our hands interlocked as we held each other close. Gazing into each other's eyes, we waltzed around the dance floor. Warmth filled my heart. I had everything I ever wanted.

About The Author

LAURA DALEO is a multi-genre author, specializing in Dark Fantasy, Urban Fantasy, Supernatural fiction, Science Fiction, and Young Adult Fiction. Immortal Kiss, her best-known vampire series, explores the Egyptian pantheon that gave rise to vampires. Currently, she is working on her eighth book, I am Wolf, an urban fantasy.

A native of San Diego, California, Laura now lives in Tucson, Arizona with her two dogs, Rose and Cooper.